Welcome to the new collection of Harlequin
Presents!

Don't miss contributions from favorite authors
Michelle Reid, Kim Lawrence and Susan Napier,
as well as the second part of Jane Porter's
THE DESERT KINGS series, Lucy Gordon's
passionate Italian, Chantelle Shaw's Tuscan
tycoon and Jennie Lucas's sexy Spaniard! And
look out for Trish Wylie's brilliant debut
Presents book, *Her Bedroom Surrender!*

We'd love to hear what you think about Harlequin
Presents. E-mail us at Presents@hmb.co.uk or join
in the discussions at www.iheartpresents.com
and www.sensationalromance.blogspot.com,
where you'll also find more information about
books and authors!

THE DESERT KINGS

Blood brothers, hot-blooded lovers—
who will they take as their queens?

These Arabian brothers stand majestically on a
desert horizon, silhouetted against sand dunes
by the white-hot sun. The sheikhs are blood
brothers, rulers of all they survey. But though
used to impossible wealth and luxury, they also
thrive on the barbaric beauty of their kingdom.
Are there women with spirit enough to tame
these hard, proud kings and become their
lifelong queens?

Jane Porter and Harlequin Presents bring you:
THE DESERT KINGS

Last month you read:
The Sheikh's Chosen Queen

Available this month:
King of the Desert, Captive Bride

Sheikh Khalid Fehr may be the youngest of
the royal brothers, but it makes him no less
passionate and powerful—he lives and breathes
for the desert. He'll give his darkened soul to the
woman who captures it!

Look on Jane's Web site for more about
THE DESERT KINGS!

Jane Porter

KING OF THE DESERT, CAPTIVE BRIDE

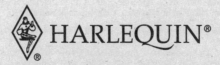

TORONTO • NEW YORK • LONDON
AMSTERDAM • PARIS • SYDNEY • HAMBURG
STOCKHOLM • ATHENS • TOKYO • MILAN • MADRID
PRAGUE • WARSAW • BUDAPEST • AUCKLAND

ISBN-13: 978-0-373-12725-2
ISBN-10:   0-373-12725-1

KING OF THE DESERT, CAPTIVE BRIDE

First North American Publication 2008.

Copyright © 2008 by Jane Porter.

This edition published by arrangement with Harlequin Books S.A.

® and TM are trademarks of the publisher. Trademarks indicated with ® are registered in the United States Patent and Trademark Office, the Canadian Trade Marks Office and in other countries.

www.eHarlequin.com

Printed in U.S.A.

All about the author...
Jane Porter

Born in Visalia, California, I'm a small-town girl at heart.
As a little girl I spent hours on my bed, staring out the
window, dreaming of far-off places, fearless knights and
happy-ever-after endings. In my imagination I was never
the geeky bookworm with the thick Coke-bottle glasses,
but a princess, a magical fairy, a Joan-of-Arc crusader.

My parents fed my imagination by taking our family to
Europe for a year when I was thirteen. The year away
changed me, and overseas I discovered a huge and
wonderful world with different cultures and customs.
I loved everything about Europe, but felt especially
passionate about Italy and those gorgeous Italian men
(no wonder my very first Harlequin Presents hero was
Italian).

I confess, after that incredible year in Europe, the travel
bug bit, and I spent much of my school years abroad,
studying in South Africa, Japan and Ireland.

After my years of traveling and studying I had to settle
down and earn a living. With my bachelor's degree from
UCLA in American studies, a program that combines
American literature and American history, I've worked in
sales and marketing, as well as a director of a nonprofit
foundation. Later I earned my Master's in writing from
the University of San Francisco, and taught junior and
high school English.

I now live in rugged Seattle, Washington, with my two
young sons. I never mind a rainy day, either, because
that's when I sit at my desk and write stories about far-
away places, fascinating people and, most importantly of
all, love.

Jane loves to hear from her readers. You can write to
her at P.O. Box 524, Bellevue, WA 98009, USA.

PROLOGUE

SHEIKH Khalid Fehr read the message posted on the Internet bulletin board again.

American Woman Missing in the Middle East.
Help desperately needed. My sister disappeared two weeks ago without a trace.
Her name is Olivia Morse. She's twenty-three years old, five-four, 105 pounds, blond, blue eyes. She speaks with a Southern accent and is on the shy side. If anyone has seen her or knows her whereabouts, please call or e-mail me. Her family is frantic.

In his tent, sitting at his laptop computer, Khalid reread the last sentence—*her family is frantic*—and felt a heavy weight lodge in his gut.

He knew what it was like to be frantic about a family member. He knew how it felt to be an older brother panicked about a sister. He'd once had two younger sisters and then one day they were gone.

He scrolled back through the message on the Internet bulletin board and discovered an earlier message from the same Jake Morse.

Missing American woman! If you've seen this woman please call or e-mail immediately.

There was a photo attached and Khalid clicked on the attachment and waited for the photo to open.

It finally did, although slowly due to the connection being via satellite phone, and Khalid found himself looking at a black-and-white photo that had to be a passport photo. White-blond hair. Light, light eyes. Pale, translucent skin. She was definitely pretty. But what really held his attention was her expression, the tentative smile and the look in her eyes—shy, curious, hopeful.

Hopeful.

His chest tightened and he leaned back in his chair, away from his desk.

His sister Aman used to look at the world that way. She was so much shyer than Jamila, the more outgoing twin. Aman's tenderness and quiet sense of humor always brought out the best in him, brought out the best in everyone, and when she died a week after Jamila he'd felt his heart break. His heart had never been the same.

Frowning at the computer screen, he ran his palm slowly along his jaw, the short, rough bristles biting at his skin. And again he looked into this missing Olivia's eyes and tried to imagine where she was, tried to imagine her circumstances. Was she sick, hurt, dead?

Had she been kidnapped? Murdered? Raped?

Or had she disappeared by choice? Was there someone, something, she was running from?

It was none of his business, he told himself, rising from his computer. He'd left city life and civilization behind to live in the desert, far from violence, noise and crime. He'd chosen solitude because he hated how most people lived.

But what if this were his sister?

What if Aman or Jamila had gone missing?

They wouldn't, he brusquely reminded himself. They'd been princesses—royal—and security detail had followed them everywhere.

He didn't know this Jake, didn't know anything about the man, but he could still see the words he'd written, could still hear the plea for help echo in his head.

Turning at the edge of his tent, Khalid looked back at his computer, at the enlarged black-and-white photo. Olivia Morse, twenty-three years old, five foot four, and one hundred and five pounds—if that.

With a snap of his wrist he flung the tent flap back, exited his tent and called for one of his men.

He might live in the middle of the Great Sarq Desert and he might be a nomadic sheikh, but he was still a king, one of the royal Fehrs, blessed with power, wealth and infinite connections. If anyone could locate this American, he could.

CHAPTER ONE

HE'D found her.

It'd taken three weeks, a small fortune, two private investigators, the help of Sarq's secretary of state, a lot of secret handshakes, deals and promises—as well as some threats—but at last he was going to see her.

Sheikh Khalid Fehr ducked to enter through Ozr Prison's low threshold. He was escorted past the men's wing to the women's side of the prison, the foul smell of overflowing toilets and unwashed bodies so overpowering his stomach rose in protest.

At the entrance to the women's prison wing his male guard handed him over to a female guard who examined Khalid's paperwork.

The female guard, covered head to foot by her black robe, took her time reading through his paperwork, and Khalid stifled his impatience. Ozr had the reputation for being one of the worst prisons in the world—it was a place notorious for the lack of human rights—but finally the female guard looked up, nodded curtly. "Follow me," she said.

He followed her through one low arched corridor after another, deeper beneath the old fortress which had been turned into Ozr Prison a half century ago.

As they walked through the corridors, hands reached out, and voices in Arabic, Egyptian, Farsi and even English begged for help, for mercy, for a doctor, a lawyer, anyone, anything. Ozr was the last place on earth any man would want to be. God only knew how it was for a woman, as once you entered through the prison's gates, you discovered you'd earned a one-way ticket. Once you were in, you never came out again.

One of Khalid's friends from high school had gotten into trouble in Jabal and after being arrested was tossed into Ozr was never heard from again. Khalid's father, the King of Sarq, had made enquiries and then entreaties on his son's friend's behalf all to no avail.

Jabal, bordered by four countries including Egypt and Sarq, remained a dangerous dictator state, with international travel warnings in place, warnings that Olivia Morse had obviously ignored.

The guard stopped before a cell that was empty except for a woman sitting on a narrow cot, her knees drawn to her chest, wisps of blond hair escaping from her black veil.

Olivia.

Khalid's chest tightened, a visceral reaction to seeing her for the first time.

In her passport photo she'd been pretty, fresh-faced, a hopeful light in her blue eyes. But the young woman sitting inside the cell didn't look like the photo anymore. The woman inside the cell appeared vacant, even half-dead.

"Olivia Morse," he asked, stepping toward the bars.

Her head briefly lifted but she didn't look at him.

"You are Miss Olivia Morse, aren't you?" he persisted, his voice pitched low.

Liv sat on the cot, legs pulled up against her, her arms wrapped tightly around her knees, trying to make herself smaller.

Maybe she wasn't really here, and maybe there wasn't another bad man standing outside her cell demanding information, threatening another interrogation, interrogations that always ended with a beating.

Didn't they understand yet that she had no answers? Didn't they understand she was as confused as they were? She'd been had. Duped. Destroyed.

Liv closed her eyes, bent her head and pressed her forehead against the bony curve of her knees. Maybe if she just kept her eyes closed she'd disappear. Dissolve. Wake up in Alabama again.

God, she missed home. God, she missed Jake and Mom and everyone.

She should have never dreamed of pyramids and beautiful waves of sand, shouldn't have wanted to ride a camel or explore the ancient tombs.

She should have been happy staying home. She should have been happy just being a travel agent, booking other people's exotic vacations.

"Olivia."

The man spoke her name quietly, urgently, and fear rose up in her, fear that something bad was going to happen again.

Turning her head away, she choked in broken Arabic, Arabic she'd learned to protect herself from another blow during the endless interrogations, "I don't know. I don't know who she was—"

"We'll discuss the charges later," he interrupted, speaking flawless English, English without a hint of an accent. "There are a few things we need to settle first."

Liv shivered. The fact that he spoke English only made her more afraid, and fear and fatigue were the only things she understood anymore.

"If I knew who she was, I'd tell you, I would. Because I want to go home—" She broke off, took a quick, unsteady breath, exhausted from the interrogations. The guards came for her at all hours of the night and then they'd skip her meals, trying to break her, trying to get the information they wanted. "I want to help you. I'm trying to help you. Believe me."

"I do," he said almost gently, and his tone, so different from the others, was her undoing.

Scalding tears filled her eyes, tears so hot they stung and burned as if filled with salt and sand.

Reaching up, she swiftly wiped her eyes dry. "I want to go home," she whispered, her voice shaky.

"And I want to see you return home."

No one had said that to her since she arrived. No one had given her the slightest bit of hope that she'd ever leave this horrible place.

Liv slowly turned her head and looked at him. The corridor was dark, shadowy, but the shadows couldn't hide his height or size. He wasn't a small man, or a stout man, not like the ones who'd interrogated her before. He was considerably younger, too.

He was robed, but his robe was black and embroidered heavily with gold. His head covering was white, pristine-white, and while the cloth concealed much of his hair it only served to emphasize his hard, strong features.

"I'm here to get you out," he continued, "but we don't have much time."

Torn between hope and dread, Liv clutched her knees to her chest, her thin back robe rough against her skin. All of her clothes had been confiscated with the rest of her things at the time of her arrest. In place of her skirts and jeans and T-shirts she'd been given this robe, and the thin, stiff linen garment she wore beneath the robe, which was little more than a slip. "Who sent you?"

The man's expression was neither friendly nor encouraging. "Your brother."

"Jake?"

"He asked me to check on you."

She lurched to her feet and then grabbed the wall for support. "Jake knows I'm here?"

"Jake knows I'm looking for you."

Liv exhaled in a dizzy rush, her fingers pressed to the damp stone wall. "They said I'd never leave here. They said I'd never get out, not until I confessed, and gave up the names of the others."

"They didn't know you were connected to powerful people," he replied.

Liv blinked, her head swimming. "Am I?"

"You are now."

She moved to the front of the cell and grabbed the bars. "How? Why?"

"I am Sheikh Khalid Fehr, and I'm here representing the royal family of Sarq."

"Sarq borders Jabal," she said.

"And Egypt," he answered. "It will be a diplomatic feat to get you out of here today, and time is short. I need to have the paperwork finalized, but I will return—"

"No!" Liv didn't mean to shout, she hadn't intended her voice to be loud at all, but panic melted her bones, turning her blood to ice. "No," she said more softly. "Please. Don't leave me here."

"It's just for a few minutes, maybe a half hour at the most—"

"No," she begged, her voice breaking, her hand snaking through the bars of the prison cell to clasp the sleeve of his robe. "Don't leave me."

For a long moment he said nothing, just stared down at her hand, his thick black lashes fanning the hard thrust of cheekbone, his skin the color of burnished gold. "They won't free you without my completing the necessary paperwork."

Her fingers tightened in his robe. "Don't go."

"I'll be back, I promise."

"I'm afraid here," she whispered. "I'm afraid of the guards. I'm afraid of the dark. I'm afraid of what happens when prisoners disappear." Her gaze clung to his, desperate, pleading. "The prisoners don't come back sometimes. They don't and I hear screaming, terrible screaming."

"I'm only going down the hall," he said. "I will be back soon."

"But they won't let you back. They won't. I know how this

place works. The American ambassador came once and he never returned."

"There is no American ambassador in Jabal," he answered. "It was a trick they played on you, a trick to try to break you."

She gripped his robe tighter. "Are you a trick, too?"

Deep grooves bracketed his mouth. For a long moment he didn't speak and then when he did, his voice dropped, deepened. "It depends on your definition of a trick."

An icy shaft chilled her. She jerked her head up, stared at him, stared hard as if she could somehow see the truth. "I don't know what to believe anymore."

"Just know I will be back. As soon as I can."

"Don't forget me," she whispered.

"I won't, and I will be back sooner than you think."

She couldn't look away from his eyes, couldn't look away in case he was making promises he didn't intend to keep. She'd been duped once more. She was beginning to think she'd never leave Ozr, never see her family again. "What if they take me away first?"

"They won't."

"They have other entrances, and different rooms. They might take me—"

"They won't."

"How do you know?"

His gaze fell to rest again on her hand, where it clutched his sleeve. "They'd be fools to try that now, with me here. They know I've seen you, they know we've spoken."

She nodded stiffly, her insides cold. She heard his words but they did little to comfort. She'd been here too long, seen too much. The guards did what they wanted when they wanted without fear of retribution.

He pulled free and was gone, disappearing down the dark corridor and all she could think as he walked away was *Come back. Come back. Please.*

* * *

Although the wait seemed endless, the sheikh did return, and with him were two prison officials.

She didn't know what to think when one of the officials unlocked her cell door and called her forward. But once the door was open, she didn't hesitate, moving quickly towards Sheikh Fehr, blindly putting her trust in him. But what choice did she have? She couldn't stay here. Anything would be better than Ozr.

Liv walked close to Sheikh Fehr back through the narrow tunnels and out the door into the dazzling sunshine. It was astonishingly hot out, and bright, and the fierce light sent her reeling backward, her legs crumpling beneath her.

Sheikh Fehr was there as she stumbled, swooping to catch her before she fell to the stone steps.

Liv had instinctively thrown her arm out to break the fall and her hand ended up being crushed to Sheikh Fehr's chest, her palm flat against his hard body, his chest a thick, dense plane of muscle.

"Oh," she choked, her fingers lifting sharply, and yet she couldn't move her hand away, her arm trapped, locked, between his broad chest and her body.

"Did you twist your ankle?" he asked, his voice so deep and husky that it made her think of the sun-drenched pyramids with their elaborate hidden treasures.

She shook her head and struggled to free herself, needing to be on her own feet again and away from this dark, silent man who filled her with both awe and terror.

"It's just so sunny," she answered unsteadily.

He placed her on her feet even as he kept one hand on the small of her back. With his other hand he removed his sunglasses and put them on her face, carefully sliding the glasses onto her nose. "You haven't been outside in a while."

It was a statement, not a question, and Liv didn't know if it was the sudden and strange intimacy of being so close to this

fiercely intimidating man or the intensity of the sun, but she felt
weak all over again, her legs like jelly beneath her.

Dipping her head, the glasses, which had already been too
big for her small face, slid to the tip of her nose. "You'd better
take them," she said, reaching up to remove them. "They're too
big for me."

But Sheikh Fehr didn't take the sunglasses. Instead he returned
them to her face and firmly pushed the frame onto the bridge of
her nose. "They might be big but they'll give your eyes a chance
to adjust," he said flatly, his flinty tone discouraging argument,
even as a series of dark cars appeared, heading toward them.

A group of robed men emerged from one of the cars and Liv
shrank closer to Sheikh Fehr's side, moving so close she could
feel his solid frame and the warmth emanating from his body.

He extended a protective arm, keeping her there at his side.
"Do not fear. They are my men and they're here to make sure
we get to the airport safely."

She nodded but her fear and worry didn't go away, and
wouldn't until she was back home with Jake and her mom. There
was too much here that felt foreign and unfamiliar. She'd wanted
the unfamiliar, it's why she'd traveled to Middle East in the first
place, but she hadn't expected problems, nor danger, not like this.

She'd chosen Egypt and Morocco because they looked
unique and picturesque in the travel brochures. She'd poured
over the travel brochures, too, lingering over photos of the
pyramids in the late afternoon sun, camels setting across the
desert at sunset, and treasures and artifacts on display at the
Egyptian Museum in Cairo.

She'd read and reread the itineraries of the Nile cruises,
imagining stopping at each of the different ports with a different temple and excursion for every day. She'd shop in the souks,
purchase practical wool rugs, buy kebabs from the street
vendors and have the adventure of a lifetime.

She'd never seriously considered the possibility of getting

into trouble. But then, she'd never been in trouble before. Liv had always been the good girl, the one that followed all the rules and did everything she was told.

One of Sheikh Fehr's guards opened the back door of the tinted-windowed sedan, and Liv turned to Sheikh Fehr, her gaze searching the hard, expressionless features. She was putting her life in his hands and she didn't even know him. "Can I trust you?" she asked, her voice all but inaudible.

His dark eyes bored into hers, his high cheekbones creating shadowed hollows above a firm, unsmiling mouth. "Perhaps I should be the one to ask that question. I've put my name, and my reputation, on the line for you. Can I trust you, Olivia Morse?"

Something in his dark, shuttered gaze sent shivers racing through her. She had the distinct feeling she was dealing with an altogether different sort of man than she'd ever dealt with before. The problem was, her experience with men was limited, and the one man she was close to—her brother, Jake—was as uncomplicated as a man could be.

Sheikh Fehr, on the other hand, struck her as quite complicated.

"Yes. Of course you can trust me," she answered huskily, trying to ignore the sudden rush of butterflies in her middle.

"Then we should go," he answered, gesturing to the open car door, "because you're not safe here, and you won't be safe until we reach my country."

In the close confines of the car, Liv dipped her head, tucking dirty blond hair back behind her ears. She was filthy, and was certain she smelled even worse. She craved a shower or bath, had never wanted to bathe as much as she did right now.

"I'm sorry," she said, realizing that the sheikh was watching her as the car sped along the road through the desolate countryside to the capital. "I know I'm in desperate need of a shower…." Her voice drifted off apologetically.

"I was thinking that your brother will be so glad when you call him later."

"Yes," Liv agreed, eyes suddenly stinging as intense emotion rushed through her. "I was beginning to lose hope that I'd ever get out of there."

"You're lucky," Khalid answered. "Most don't."

"Why don't they?"

"They don't have the power."

"I didn't have any power," she said, voice soft.

"No. But I did."

"You've done this before…helped people like me?"

"Yes."

Her lips parted to ask him more, to find out who he was, and why he'd risk his own safety to help others, but he'd turned his head away to stare out the tinted window and the hard set of his features discouraged further conversation.

Almost everything about him discouraged conversation. Dark, big and powerfully built, she found him incredibly intimidating.

Sheikh Fehr had towered over her when they stood side by side waiting for the car and she had to believe he was at least six feet tall, if not taller. He was also quite broad-shouldered, with an athletic build. His skin was deeply tanned, with strong, rugged features that spoke of sun and wind and hot, stinging sand.

"We're approaching Hafel, the capital city of Jabal," Sheikh Fehr said. "Did you see any of the city before your arrest?"

Liv shook her head and, glancing down at her lap, she glimpsed the inside of her wrist where yellow and blue bruises remained. She also had more bruises high on her arms, but her robe covered those. "I never got as far as Hafel."

"Where were you arrested?"

"On the main road between the border and Hafel." She made a faint sound, part misery, part disbelief. "One moment I was on the bus, and the next I was on my way to Ozr."

When the sheikh didn't answer Liv looked up at him. "Are we stopping in Hafel now?"

"No," Khalid answered as the capital city, a city thousands of years old, appeared before them. The city boasted relatively new modern office buildings that rose over and between crumbling Roman ruins. "Although it's a fascinating city, a city most of the Western world knows nothing about."

"Have you spent much time here?" she asked.

"Once upon a time."

"What changed?"

"Everything." He hesitated. "When I was a boy my father had a close friendship with the Jabal king, but the king was overthrown twenty years ago and the country is ruled by someone far different now." His lips twisted cynically. "This is the first time I've been here in four years and until last night, I wasn't even sure they'd allow me in."

"Why not?"

"I get people out of prison, whisking them off to safer places. The government here doesn't like it." He shrugged. "They don't like me."

Liv's stomach did a peculiar somersault. "So why did they let you in?"

He briefly glanced out the window, his shoulders shifting carelessly before glancing back at her. "I paid off several high-up officials."

Drawing a quick breath she felt her stomach fall again and wondered if she'd ever feel safe again. "You *bribed* them?"

"Didn't have much of a choice." He dark eyes rested on her face, his expression grim. "It was either that, or allow you to go before the Ozr Prison judge in two days' time, and believe me, you wouldn't have survived the sentence."

Liv bit her lip and looked away, out the window. They were approaching the city center, which was far more cramped than the modern neighborhoods. Smoke rose from food stands on the street corners. "It would have been harsh," she said.

"It would have been deadly," he agreed.

"And I just wanted to have an adventure," she said, her voice low. "I never imagined this nightmare."

The driver slowed, then braked to a complete stop. The sheikh's wireless phone suddenly rang and he answered it, his eyes on the line of police cars ahead.

"The nightmare," he said, echoing her words as he hung up the phone, "isn't over yet."

Liv leaned forward to get a look at the police officers ahead. "What's happening?"

"We're to be questioned," he answered shortly, his features hardening. Turning his head, he looked at her, a close, ruthless inspection that was as thorough as it was critical.

"Pull your headscarf forward," he directed. "Hide all your hair and wrap the fabric across your mouth and nose so that as much of your face is covered as possible." He retrieved the sunglasses from the seat and handed them to her. "And keep these on. Don't take them off unless I tell you to." Then he opened the car door and stepped out, slamming it shut behind him.

CHAPTER TWO

THE nightmare isn't over yet.

Sheikh Fehr's words rang in her ears as he walked from the car. The driver had locked the car doors the moment the sheikh left the vehicle and she watched Sheikh Fehr now, heart in her throat, as a group of uniformed officers approached him.

From inside the car she could hear their muffled voices outside. The officers practically surrounded the sheikh, but he appeared unruffled.

They were speaking Arabic and she understood nothing of what they were saying other than there seemed to be a problem, and from the way the officers kept gesturing to the car, their voices growing louder, she had a sick feeling that the conversation had something to do with her.

Several long minutes passed and then Sheikh Fehr turned to the car and opened the back door. Liv ducked her head as the officers crowded around to get a look inside. Terrified, she kept her head down, her eyes closed behind the oversized pair of sunglasses.

After what seemed like eternity the car door slammed shut and shortly after the sheikh climbed back in the car. The chauffeur immediately started the ignition and pulled away.

Liv nervously laced and unlaced her fingers. "Is everything okay?" she asked, as they left the narrower, old city streets behind for the wide boulevard that ran along the North Africa coast.

"Yes."

When it became clear he didn't intend to say more she added, "What did they want?"

"They wanted to know if I'd legally entered their country and if I'd done anything illegal while here."

"Have you?"

"No and yes, but that's not what I told them. I couldn't tell them that or you'd be in one of their cars heading straight back to Ozr."

"So what did you tell them instead?"

He hesitated a moment, then plucked the sunglasses from her face, calmly pocketing them inside his robe. "That I was escorting a female member of my family home."

But he wasn't, she thought, her uneasiness growing. "Did they believe you?"

His expression turned mocking. "They know who I am, and they saw I had the proper paperwork. There wasn't much they could do at that point."

He was setting her newly heightened inner alarm, the one that should have been working when she agreed to carry Elsie's bag in her backpack.

Her inner alarm hadn't been attuned to danger then, but it was now, and Liv knew from Sheikh Fehr's tone, as well as his evasive answers, that there was something he wasn't telling her. Something wasn't right. She didn't know what it was and she very much wanted to know. "The officers were upset about something," she persisted.

He shrugged. "It's a cultural thing."

She leaned forward. "Tell me."

"We're a man and woman traveling alone together."

"So?"

"We're not actually related, which is illegal in Jabal."

Liv sat back against the seat, her fingers curling into her palms. "So they could rearrest me," she whispered.

"Not if we get out of here first."

They reached the small business airport in less than thirty minutes, the airport built on the outskirts of the capital city. The chauffeur drove them through the airport gates and right out onto the deserted tarmac, pulling close to the jet's stairs.

The jet was long, sleek and narrow, the body a shiny silver with a discrete gold-and-black emblem on the tail. Sheikh Fehr walked Olivia to the jet's stairs. "Go ahead and board," he told her. "I need to speak with the pilot about our flight plan."

She nodded and, holding on to the handrail, climbed the steps. A flight attendant greeted Liv as she entered the plane.

"We'll be leaving soon," the flight attendant said, leading Liv to the grouping of four enormous club-style leather chairs that made up one of the plane's sitting areas. "Do you have any bags or luggage for me to stow?"

Liv shook her head as she sat down. "I don't have…anything," she said, reaching for the seat belt.

"So your luggage has been sent ahead?" the flight attendant asked.

"Unfortunately, I've lost everything," Liv answered, and suddenly, remembering how she'd been callously stripped and searched, she shivered. They'd confiscated everything that first night. Her backpack, her passport, her clothes, her makeup bag. All of it. The only thing she had was what she wore, and even that was a prison-issued robe and headscarf.

The flight attendant saw Liv shiver. "Cold?"

"A little," Liv admitted, still chilled from the weeks and weeks in the dark, dank cell. It'd been so awful, so unbelievable. She still couldn't understand how she'd ended up at Ozr. She'd never broken a law in her life—well, except for driving over the speed limit, and even then, it had been five miles over the limit, not twenty.

"Would you like a blanket?"

"Please." Liv smiled gratefully.

"Poor thing. Have you been sick?" the flight attendant asked sympathetically as she crossed to the wood-paneled cabinet and retrieved an ivory cashmere throw and small pillow, the ivory blanket the same color as the supple leather seats.

Returning, the flight attendant unfolded the blanket and draped it across Liv's legs. "And just between you and me, I think the air conditioner is a little too efficient. Now, how about something warm to drink? Coffee, tea?"

"Coffee, with milk and sugar. If that's not too much trouble."

"None at all."

The flight attendant disappeared into the jet's galley kitchen and Liv sank deeper into her seat. This was surreal, she thought, tugging the blanket up to her shoulders. An hour ago she was still locked up in Ozr and now here she was, on a private jet, being waited on hand and foot.

While Liv sipped her coffee on the plane, Khalid joined his pilot in the final preflight inspection.

"We've a change of plans," Khalid told the pilot.

The pilot looked up from his clipboard. "We're low on petrol. The airport refused our request to refuel."

"I'm not surprised. We had a little problem on the way here."

"Is that why we're not going straight to Sarq?"

Khalid nodded. "Can't risk involving my brother in this. There's enough tension between Sarq and Jabal already. I won't drag Sharif, or my people, into an international incident."

The pilot's attention was suddenly caught by a line of cars on the horizon. "Police," he said, nodding at the line of cars racing toward them. "Are they coming for you?"

"That, or my guest, or us both," Khalid replied, dispassionately watching the cars grow closer.

The pilot patted the side of the plane. "Then maybe it's time to go."

Liv looked up as Sheikh Fehr and the pilot boarded, the pilot drawing the folding stairs up and then securing the door. Sheikh Fehr stopped to speak to the flight attendant and then continued down the aisle to take a seat across from Liv.

"Are you not feeling well?" he asked Liv, seeing the blanket wrapped around her.

"I was cold," she answered, feeling the engine turn on, a low vibration that hummed through the entire plane.

Sheikh Fehr's eyes narrowed as he inspected her. "You are quite pale. I wonder if you're coming down sick."

"I'm not sick. Just chilly. But I'm getting warmer." She started to fold the blanket up, but the sheikh put out a hand to stop her.

"Don't," he said. "If the blanket is keeping you warm, there's no need to put it away."

As the jet began to taxi toward the runway, she resettled the blanket on her lap and glanced at him from beneath her lashes. Against his white head-covering, his skin was a tawny gold, while his eyebrows were inky slashes above long-lashed eyes the color of bittersweet chocolate.

His features were almost too angular, too strong. His forehead was high, his cheekbones were prominent, even his nose was a trifle too long. It should have made him unattractive. Instead it gave him a rugged, and very primitive, appeal.

As she looked at him, a window behind his shoulder, she caught sight of a flashing red-and-blue light.

Her eyes widened as she spotted the line of cars trailing the jet.

The sheikh glanced out the window. "Police," he said matter-of-factly.

She looked at him, her stomach tumbling, the fear returning. "What do they want now?"

"Us," he answered.

Us, she repeated silently, as the jet began racing down the runway, faster and faster until they were off the ground and soaring up, up, into the air.

Liv sat glued to the window.

Within ten minutes they had lifted high above the congested streets of the capital, and as they climbed higher, green fields came into view before the green faded to a khaki gold, and then even the gold hue faded, leaving just pale khaki.

"What happened in Ozr?" Sheikh Fehr asked abruptly. "What did they do to you?"

Liv jerked her attention away from the landscape below. "Nothing," she answered quickly, too quickly, and from the creasing of the sheikh's eyes, she knew he knew it, too.

"Ozr isn't a nice place," he said. "I can't imagine they were nice to you."

She suddenly pictured her life of the past four long weeks. The terrible food, the lack of sunlight, the lack of exercise, the taunts, the accusations and the endless middle-of-the-night interrogations. "I'm here now."

His jaw tightened. "Barely," he answered quietly, his gaze meeting hers.

She suppressed a shiver and turned away, unable to hold his intense gaze, or dwell on her weeks in Ozr. She was out now. That's what mattered. She was out and soon she'd be going home.

"The view is beautiful from here," she said, determinedly turning her attention to the landscape below.

He gestured toward the stretch of brown and beige beneath them. "That's the Great Sarq Desert. It begins in Southern Jabal and stretches through much of Sarq, my country, and is one of the largest deserts in Northern Africa, consisting of thousands of miles."

"I've read quite a bit about the Great Sarq Desert," she said shyly but eagerly. "I read that thousands of years ago the desert was once a lush tropical landscape, that there are elaborate rock paintings in the mountains depicting everyday life. Is that true?"

He nodded. "Yes, and scattered oases are all that's left of that ancient tropical landscape."

"Oases used by traders and their caravans," she added, her gaze glued to the empty plains below. "Before the trip I was reading a book on the area, and it said that in ancient civilization the desert here was the corridor that linked Africa with the coast, and the world beyond. Everyone utilized the desert corridor. The Romans, the Phoenicians, as well as the early Greek colonists—" She broke off, flushing. "But of course you know all that. It's just…new…to me."

The look her gave her was frankly appraising. "I didn't know American women cared about geography so far from their own homes."

Her eyebrows lifted. "You can't judge America, or Americans, by what you read in the news."

"No?" he mocked.

"No." She held her breath for a moment, battling her temper. "Just like it'd be unfair of me to judge all the countries in this area by what happened to me in Ozr."

The rest of the flight passed in silence. Liv tried to blank her mind, desperate to ignore the questions and worrying thoughts racing through her head. She leaned back in her chair and turned her attention to the landscape below and for a short while, it provided the much-needed distraction.

The vast desert, with its contrasting hues of tan and orange, burnt amber and rust, maroon and even a few shades of purple, held her captivated as flat expanses of sand gave way to gently rising sand dunes, which led to even higher hills. She'd never thought the desert could have so many contrasting colors. It was breathtakingly beautiful.

Before long the hills completely disappeared and desert sand gave way to the Red Sea, the deep turquoise colors a vivid contrast to the view they had left behind. Liv was again craning her head to see out the window as they flew over the coast of the African continent. Brilliant blue water sparkled below as it suddenly dawned on her that they weren't headed to Sarq but a different destination.

It had to be Dubai, she thought. It was one of the most cosmopolitan cities in the Middle East and a place very far removed from Jabal. "Are we headed to Dubai?" she asked, as the plane tilted slightly, giving her a wider view of the Arabian Peninsula looming on the horizon.

"No, we're going to Baraka. I have friends there and you'd be safe. But tell me, how is it that a girl from a small Southern town knows so much about the Middle East?"

"I pour over travel brochures all day," she said, but from his expression she could see he didn't understand. "I'm a travel agent," she added.

"So you're a world traveler."

She shook her head regretfully. "No. I don't usually travel. I just book trips for other people. This is my first real trip. Until now I'd never been out of the U.S."

Suddenly the nose of the plane tipped and they seemed to be changing direction again. Sheikh Fehr frowned and reached for his seat belt. The flight attendant moved toward them at the same time.

She knelt at his side and spoke quietly in Arabic. "The pilot said we've a problem. We're dangerously low on petrol. We need to land almost immediately. Fortunately we've been given permission to land in Cairo."

"Good. Thank you," Khalid answered, glancing at Olivia, knowing that things were beginning to get a little more complicated than he liked.

By being diverted at the last minute from Baraka to Egypt he wouldn't be able to process Olivia swiftly. He'd planned on having her checked out by a doctor then put on a private jet to New York tonight. Instead they were landing in Cairo, which meant they'd need to find a place to stay, and since he couldn't use his preferred pilot and jet, nor the doctor he normally used, he'd need to find another way to get her quickly and quietly attended to. Unfortunately, it wouldn't be today, or tonight.

Olivia turned just then to look at him, her blue eyes wide, almost pinched, in her pale oval face. She was still wearing her headscarf, but the fabric was loose around her neck, exposing her delicate features.

"What's wrong?" she asked, fear in her voice, the same fear that made her eyes turn to lapis.

"We've had a change of plans," he answered.

Her forehead creased. "*Another?* Why? What's happened?"

"Out of petrol, or as you Americans call it, gas. So we're landing in Egypt instead of Baraka."

He wasn't sure what he expected, but her sudden smile stunned her, her blue eyes widening with excitement. "Egypt?" she repeated. "I was on my way to Egypt when I was arrested. Will we have time to see the pyramids in Giza?"

"Unfortunately not. We'll be landing and hopefully taking off as soon as we refuel. We need to get to Baraka tonight."

Her gaze searched his as if trying to see what he wasn't telling her. "Why?"

"You want to go home, don't you?"

She nodded slowly, clearly puzzled. "But if we don't make it out tonight, we'll just go tomorrow, right?"

He wasn't ready to tell her that things were a lot more complicated than she knew.

For the past ten years he'd operated his version of an underground railroad. He specialized in rescuing innocent people and he'd enlisted some powerful friends to help him. People like Sheikh Kalen Nuri, the younger brother of Baraka's King Malik Nuri, and Sheikh Tair, leader of the independent state Ouaha.

In the past few years Kalen and Tair had helped him with dozens of impossible rescues, and they'd pledged to help with Olivia's, but first they had to get to Baraka.

"We want to reach Baraka tonight," he said tersely, unwilling to give up his initial goal. "I need to make a few calls," he added, rising from his seat. "Relax, try to get a little sleep. I will be able to tell you more once we're on the ground."

Twenty minutes later they touched down, the jet landing so smoothly that Liv didn't even realize they were on the ground until the pilot began to brake, slowing the jet's speed.

After taxiing to the terminal the jet sat on the tarmac, not far from the executive terminal. Khalid didn't appear and the pilot hadn't emerged from the cockpit.

Liv, seeing the flight attendant on the plane phone, flagged her down. "Are we refueling?" she asked.

But before the flight attendant could answer, Sheikh Fehr walked from the cockpit back to Liv's seat.

"We're staying in Cairo tonight," he said. "I've a car waiting. Let's go."

Liv shot him an uneasy glance. He was angry. She felt his tension wash over her in dark brooding waves. Something had happened. Something not good.

"What's wrong?" she asked, unbuckling her seat belt and rising to her feet. From her window she could see a black car outside, waiting not far from the plane.

"We can talk later," he answered, extending a hand, his black robe with the gold embroidery swirling. "Come. Traffic will be heavy. We need to go."

She put her fingers in his, shuddering at the sharp hot spark that passed between them. She wanted very much to take her hand back but was afraid of upsetting him.

Once seated in the car, their driver sped on and off highways and Liv marveled at the way Sheikh Fehr traveled.

She'd never met anyone who owned his own jet and employed his own pilot and flight crew. Even though she worked in the travel industry, she thought of flying as booking a ticket on a commercial airline, then going to a crowded airport for an endless wait in a long security line. Maybe it was just the U.S., but modern travel meant canceled flights, missed connections, lost luggage, no meal service and irritated flight attendants. In short, flying was far from luxurious, and definitely not glamorous. But Sheikh Fehr's jet was sumptuous, as was his fleet of cars.

The fact that he had access to a fleet of cars in different countries, never mind the security, made her wonder about him, and his power.

What kind of man could accomplish the things he did?

What kind of man risked life and limb for a stranger?

Unless he did it for money.

Hiding her worry, she shot another glance his way. Could he be a mercenary of sorts?

The thought made her skin crawl, nearly as much as her disgusting black prison-issued robe and lank headscarf did.

Self-consciously she reached up and touched the headscarf she still wore. The flight attendant hadn't worn one and Liv wondered now if it was still necessary. "Can I take this off?" she asked.

"Please. In Jabal we didn't have a choice, but here in Egypt, and my country of Sarq, it's optional."

"Some women want to wear the veil?"

"They view it as protection, shielding them from leering eyes and inappropriate advances." His gaze swept over her. "You will need something else to wear though. That's obviously a prison-issued robe."

Liv plucked at her robe's stiff, coarse fabric. "I can't stand this thing," she confessed, her voice dropping. "It's all I've worn since they arrested me and I hate it. I never want to put it on again."

"You won't have to. And once we're at the hotel, I'll make sure the robe's properly disposed of."

"Thank you." Tears inexplicably burned the backs of her eyes and she had to squeeze her eyes shut to hold the emotion in. She was just tired. Overwhelmed by the day. There was no reason to cry. She'd be home soon. If not tonight, then tomorrow. And everything would be all right. She just needed to call her mom, or Jake. Once she heard their voices she knew she'd be okay.

"So we are staying in Cairo overnight?" she asked.

"Yes."

"Why?"

He shifted, shoulders shrugging impatiently. "My pilot was concerned about the plane. He was afraid there was a fuel leak and wanted it checked out before we flew again."

"Sensible."

"Yes."

But from his tone, she knew the sheikh didn't agree and she was hit with another wave of homesickness. She was tired of strangers, tired of short-tempered men and women. She just wanted to go home. Back to the people who knew her and loved her, and back to people she loved.

"Can I call my brother now?" she asked, her voice wobbly with the threat of tears.

"Maybe we should wait a little longer, until you've seen the doctor."

His words were a one-two punch and Liv stiffened. "A doctor? Why?"

"It's routine. Standard practice whenever someone's been released—"

"How often *do* you do this?" she interrupted.

"Often enough to know that you need to be checked out and cleared for travel."

"But I'm fine," she insisted. She didn't want anyone touching her, didn't want anyone looking at her or poking at her or coming near her. She'd had enough of that at Ozr. "I'm fine."

His dark gaze pierced her. "It's not an option, Miss Morse." His tone hardened. "You have to. I can't take any chances.

You've been in Ozr for weeks. The place is a breeding ground for all sorts of diseases."

"I doubt I've caught anything and if I have, I'll deal with it at home." *With my doctor*, she silently, furiously added.

Sheikh Fehr might have rescued her from Ozr, but she couldn't completely trust him. She didn't trust anyone here anymore. These countries and cultures were far too different from hers.

Her longing for home had become an endless ache inside her. She missed her mom and brother. She wanted her mother's delicious Sunday pot roast, and her melt-in-your-mouth mashed potatoes and the best brown gravy in the world.

She wanted Pierceville with its sleepy Main Street and big oak trees and the old Fox theater where they still showed movies. She missed Main Street's angled parking and the drugstore on the corner and the two bakeries with their cake displays in the window.

"You won't be given permission to leave the country if you're not cleared for travel." He spoke slowly to make sure he was heard. "And if you're not cleared for travel, you don't go home."

Home.

That word she understood, that word cut through her fog of misery.

Turning away to hide the shimmer of tears, Liv stared out the car window, the stream of traffic outside a blur.

"Whose rule is that?" she asked thickly. "Yours, or the government's?"

"Both."

Biting her lip, it crossed her mind that maybe, just maybe, she'd jumped from the frying pan into the fire.

Khalid Fehr watched Olivia turn her face away from him. She was upset but that was her choice. He had to be careful. He took tremendous risks in helping people. At the end of the day, once someone was safe and en route to their home, he wanted to go home himself, back to his beloved desert.

The desert was where he belonged.

The desert was where he found peace.

"The doctor's a personal friend," he said quietly, only able to see the back of her head, and then when the sun struck the outside of the window, it turned the glass into a mirror, giving him an almost perfect reflection of her pale, set face.

She looked lost, he thought. Gone. Like a ghost of a woman.

Her fear ate at him all over again, stirring the fury in him, the fury that was only soothed, calmed, by acts of valor.

It was ridiculous, really, this need of his to save others, this need to unite families torn apart, to return missing loved ones to those who waited, grieved.

He wasn't a hero, didn't want to be a hero, and this wasn't the life he'd ever wanted for himself. He'd loved his studies, had enjoyed his career, but that all ended when his sisters died.

Thinking of his sisters reminded him of Olivia and her brother Jake and all her family had gone through in the past five or six weeks since she disappeared. "I'm trying to help you," he said quietly.

"Then send me home," she answered, her voice breaking.

His jaw jutted. She wasn't the only one who couldn't go home yet. He couldn't, either, and he wasn't much happier about it than she was.

Anytime he took these human rights cases on, he moved swiftly, moved a person in and out in a day. These rescues always took place within twenty-four hours and then he was home again, back in his quiet world of sky and sand. Back in anonymity.

Today was different. Everything about today's rescue was different. And that didn't bode well for any of them.

CHAPTER THREE

A HALF hour later they reached the famous Mena House Hotel, a historic hotel on the outskirts of Cairo.

Liv leaned forward to get a glimpse of the historic property but saw little of the hotel's entrance with the dozen black cars lining the drive and virtually blocking the front door.

"It looks like the President of the United States has arrived," she said, staring at all the cars and security detail. "I wonder who it's for?"

"Us," he answered cryptically, as security moved toward their car, flanking the front and back.

She jerked around to look at him. "Why?"

He shrugged as the door opened.

"Your Highness," one of the men said, bowing deeply. "Welcome. The hotel is secure."

Liv didn't move. She couldn't. Her body had gone nerveless. "Who *are* you?"

"I'm Sheikh Khalid Fehr. Prince of the Great Sarq Desert."

And then it came together, all the missing pieces, all the little things that hadn't added up. Sarq. Fehr. The family name, Fehr. "Your brother is King Fehr," she whispered.

"Yes."

"You're…royalty."

His broad shoulders shifted. "I didn't ask for the job. I inherited it." And then he climbed out of the car.

They were escorted through the opulent, gilded lobby to a private elevator that glided soundlessly up to the royal suite, which occupied the entire penthouse floor.

Their suite consisted of two enormous bedrooms and ensuite baths opening off a central living area. The suite was dark, the windows curtained, but then the butler drew the curtains back and the suite was flooded with late-afternoon sunlight, and the most astonishing view of the Great Pyramid.

"Incredible," Liv murmured, standing at the window, hands pressed to the glass.

"There's a balcony in each of the bedrooms," the butler offered. "Very nice for a morning coffee or evening nightcap."

She could only nod. She didn't want to move, or be distracted. She just wanted to stand here and feast on the most amazing thing she'd ever seen.

The golden stone pyramid soared…gigantic, mythic, spectacular.

This is why she'd traveled so far from home. This is what she'd wanted to see. Ancient wonders. Relics of a glorious past.

But then Khalid Fehr spoke. "The doctor is here, Olivia."

Her insides did a quick freeze and she slowly, reluctantly turned from the window. A woman in a dark slack suit and wearing a dark scarf around her shoulders stood next to Khalid.

"I'm Dr. Nenet Hassan," the woman said briskly. "I'm a friend of Sheikh Fehr's from university. The exam won't hurt, and it won't take long, either. We'll just step into your room and get it over, shall we?"

Liv wouldn't even look at Khalid as she headed for her bedroom with Dr. Hassan close behind. She didn't want the exam, didn't need a checkup, but no one seemed to be listening.

Fortunately, the exam was as quick as Dr. Hassan had said and in less than ten minutes the physician was putting her instruments away. "You're healthy," Dr. Hassan said. "And I know you're dying for a bath so go ahead, enjoy. I'll have a word with Sheikh Fehr and see myself out."

Khalid was waiting for Nenet as she emerged from Liv's room. "Well?" he demanded.

"She has some bruises but they're not specific to any injury."

"She hasn't been beaten?" Khalid asked bluntly.

"She does have marks and the odd bruise or cut, but that's to be expected. It's a well-known fact that the female guards are far harder on the female prisoners than the male guards are on the men. They're just more aggressive, although the abuse leans toward the mental instead of the physical."

"What about drug use?" he asked.

Nenet lifted her head, and her somber brown gaze searched his. "You suspect her of using?"

"No. But you never know."

The doctor's expression remained speculative. "I didn't see needle marks, or anything else indicative of drug abuse."

"Good," he answered, turning away to look out the same window that had so completely captured Liv's imagination earlier.

"Do you really intend to marry her?" Nenet asked, catching Khalid off guard. "Or is it just another baseless rumor?"

His forehead creased and he turned from the window to look at the doctor over his shoulder. "How did you hear?"

"How did I hear? Khalid, it's all over the news! A high-ranking Jabal official announced that you'd visited his country today to bring your betrothed home." Nenet swallowed hard. "And this…this…American…she's your *betrothed*?"

None of this was supposed to be happening, Khalid thought. He was supposed to have freed Olivia from prison, zipped to Baraka in his jet, had her cleared by a doctor and then hurried onto a waiting jet provided by Kalen Nuri, and then she'd fly home and he'd fly back to the Sarq desert in his jet and it'd be finished. No naming of names, no police chases, no publicity.

"I don't know that this is an appropriate conversation for us to be having," he said flatly.

He'd once dated Nenet Hassan during his second year of graduate school, but the pressures on both of them had been intense, and then when his sisters had died, he'd broken the relationship off. Nenet had written long letters to him, saying she'd wait for him, promising he could take all the time he needed to heal, but Khalid hadn't wanted time to heal. He hadn't wanted to heal. He just wanted out. Away. Gone from the life he'd lived and the people he'd known.

"Forgive me, Khalid. Please don't be angry. I know it's not my place," Nenet added quickly, trying to ease the tension and awkward silence, "but I can't ignore what you're doing. It wouldn't be right."

"And what am I doing?" he asked even more gruffly.

"You know what you're doing. I know what you're doing. But stop. Don't. Don't sacrifice yourself for her." Grief darkened her eyes. "You aren't merely a good man, Khalid, you are a great man, and a man that has suffered enough. You owe her nothing, especially not your future, or your freedom."

In the bathroom, Liv stood in the middle of the marble tiled floor for what seemed like forever.

The bathroom was beyond decadent. The decor was reminiscent of the Great Pyramid outside, with pale ivory and gold limestone pavers on the floor and more buttery-colored limestone surrounding the deep bathtub.

A series of three glass-covered jars rested on the tub surround. She lifted each of the lids and smelled the different scented bath salts—verbena, orange blossom and hyacinth—and suddenly a lump filled her throat, making it hard to breathe.

She'd been in hell for weeks and just when she thought there was no hope, she was plucked from her cell and rushed to the airport. Now she was in this palatial suite with a palatial bath furnished with thick, plush towels and exquisitely scented bath salts and fragrant designer shampoos.

It was strange. Impossible. Overwhelming.

The transition was too much.

Leaning over the marble surround, she turned on the water. While the tub filled she stripped off her hated robe and the black sheath she wore under the robe and balled the fabric up and smashed it into the rubbish bin beneath the vanity.

Naked, she examined herself in the mirror. Even to her eyes she looked too thin, gaunt, with yellow and purple-blue bruises on her arms and legs. Turning part way, she studied her back and spotted a big fading bruise on her hip and a newer bruise on her left shoulder.

But the bruises would go and she'd recover and she'd be home. Soon. Soon, she repeated, dumping in two scoops of the verbena-scented bath salt before sliding carefully into the hot water.

The bath felt like heaven and she soaked until the water cooled, forcing her to action by shampooing and conditioning her hair.

Later, clean and wrapped in the soft white cotton sateen robe found hanging on the back of the door, Liv left the bathroom for her bedroom and then realized she didn't know what to do next. She had no clothes. She didn't feel comfortable wandering around the suite in just a robe. The conservative climate of the Middle East made her aware that she shouldn't be sharing a suite with man she didn't know.

Fresh anxiety hit and out of an old nervous habit, she began chewing her thumbnail down, chewing it to bits.

She had to go home. She needed to go home, and even thought the hotel was gorgeous, and this was probably the only time in her life that she'd ever stay in a five-star property, she couldn't enjoy it. Couldn't appreciate the high ceilings, the tall windows and the exotic decor, not when her mother and her brother were waiting for her and worrying about her.

Crossing to the table near her bed, she picked up the phone

and asked the hotel operator to put through a call to the States. The operator answered that she couldn't make the call for her, but gave Liv the international codes so Liv could dial the call from her hotel room.

Liv was scribbling the codes down when a knock sounded on her bedroom door. Her heart skipped. "Just a minute," she called, swiftly trying to dial the string of numbers, then making a mistake in the middle and having to start all over again.

"We need to talk." It was Khalid's deep voice on the other side of the door.

Fingers trembling, she finished inputting the long sequence of numbers. "Okay," she called back. "I'll be out soon."

There was a pause. "We should really talk before you call home," he said. "There are things you should know, things that you might, or might not, want your family to know."

She could hear the ring of her mother's line. Liv gripped the phone more tightly. She suddenly wanted to hear her mother's voice more than anything in the whole world.

"Olivia," Khalid continued, his deep voice unnervingly clear despite the door between them, "you don't have a passport any longer, and it could be difficult to get another issued soon. Perhaps we should discuss a way to break the news to your family without frightening them?"

She could hear the ringing on the line. Could imagine her mother looking for the phone, wondering where she'd left it this time.

Eyes smarting, emotion thick in her chest, Liv hung up before her mother could answer.

She couldn't worry her mom. She loved her too much.

Beseiged by conflicted emotions, Liv walked to the bedroom door and opened it. Khalid stood on the other side, his robe discarded in favor of exquisitely tailored European-style clothes: dark slacks, supple black leather belt, crisp long-sleeved cotton shirt the color of espresso and black leather shoes. His dark hair was cut short and sleek, emphasizing the strong lines of his face.

He didn't even look like the same person and she didn't know why his transformation felt like one more blow.

Nothing was what she'd expected. Imagined.

Nothing made sense.

Pressing her hands into her robe's pockets, she took a quick breath for courage. "Sheikh Fehr, in the car, you said to wait to call my brother until after I'd seen the doctor, and I waited. Now you tell me not to call home because I don't have a passport and I shouldn't worry my family." Her eyes met his and held. "I don't know what to believe anymore."

"Maybe we should sit down."

"I don't want to sit. I just want the truth."

"As you, yourself know, the truth is complicated."

She blinked, puzzled. "What does that mean?"

"You were charged with smuggling drugs, and the drugs were found on your person—"

"In a bag I was holding for a friend!"

He shrugged. "But it was in your backpack, in your possession, making you responsible. Complicating the truth is the fact that this 'friend' disappeared and we have no proof she ever existed."

"That's not true! I had her bag. Her cosmetics. Her toiletries."

"Who is to say they aren't yours?"

She stared up at him, appalled. "You don't believe me? You think I did it—"

"I never said that. I was just pointing out that truth isn't always what it seems, just as my freeing you, isn't quite what it seems, either."

She suddenly felt very woozy, her head starting to spin. "I'm beginning to feel dizzy."

His brows pulled in a fierce line. "I knew you were better off sitting."

Ignoring her attempt to brush him off, he put one hand to

her elbow and the other to the small of her back—a touch that scorched her even through her thick robe—and escorted her to the plump upholstered chair in the living room.

"I'm not going to break," she said breathlessly, her heart hammering unsteadily as heat washed through her. She could feel his hand despite the plush robe, could feel the press of his fingers against the dip in her spine, and it made her head spin even faster.

"I know you're not going to break," he answered, making sure she was safely ensconced in the chair before stepping away, "but you've been through a traumatic ordeal, and unfortunately, it's not over yet."

Liv stared up at him, battling to get control over her pulse and her thoughts. "I'd think the American embassy would step in now, accelerate the process of getting me home."

"They'd like to, but they work with the local government, and Jabal is lobbying very hard to have you returned to them for sentencing."

She made a soft sound of disbelief. "Can the Jabal government extradite me from here?"

"No," he answered, standing above her, arms folded, his expression downright forbidding. "At least, hopefully not."

With a trembling hand Liv pushed a damp tendril of hair away from her face, trying to sort out everything he was saying, stress and exhaustion making the task even harder than it should be. "That doesn't sound very reassuring," she said hoarsely, blinking back the sting of tears.

"It's not meant to be. You should know the truth, and the truth is, things are…unpredictable…at the moment."

His response just added to her fears. "I won't go back to Jabal," she choked. "I can't. I *can't*—"

"I know, and I wouldn't let you go back."

She looked up at him, scared, so very scared, and bundled her arms more tightly across her chest. "Why are you doing all this? Why are you helping me?"

"Your brother posted a message for help on the Internet. His message came to my attention."

Her chest felt so hot, and her emotions felt ragged. She didn't know if she could—should—believe him. "You did all this just because you saw a message on the Internet?"

"Yes."

Who did things like this? Who broke into prisons and rescued people? *"Why?"*

His shuttered gaze rested on her face, his expression as blank as the tone of his voice. "Your brother said your family was frantic." He paused for a split second before adding, "It touched me."

Her brow wrinkled as she digested his words, thinking it was odd to hear him use the word *touched* when he struck her as emotional as one of the limestone statues she'd seen carved into the wall of the Ozr fortress turned prison. "And you acted alone?"

"Yes."

"But if you weren't working with an embassy or government, how did you get me released?"

He made a rough, mocking sound. "The old-fashioned way. Power. Blackmail. Intimidation."

"Isn't that illegal?" she asked, trying to keep the horror from her voice.

"Blackmail is never pretty," he answered. "But it was you or them, and it's not as if the guards were good to you. The doctor told me she found bruises on you, bruises I'm certain you didn't inflict on yourself."

She just looked away, towards the window with the spectacular view of the pyramid.

Khalid dropped to his haunches, crouching before her, and turned her face to him. "No diplomatic measure would have ever gotten you freed from Ozr. Jabal doesn't care about diplomacy. They don't recognize diplomacy. They only recognize power and money. I did what I had to do, and I don't apologize for it. At least you're here, safe and alive."

Liv felt his fingers on her chin, felt the fierce heat in his eyes and the coiled tension in his powerful frame. She was simultaneously fascinated and terrified by the fire in his dark eyes. He intrigued her and yet intimidated her. He was hard and fierce and remote, and yet he'd also come to rescue her when no one else had, or would. "But not free," she whispered.

"Are you free to go home, back to Pierceville, Alabama? No. Are you free of the prison cell?" He hesitated for a fraction of a second and then stood again. "For now."

For now. The words echoed loudly in her head. She was free only for now.

"But money alone didn't buy your freedom," he added. "It required honor. My honor."

She gave her head a slight shake. His honor. It was such an archaic-sounding word, so old-fashioned it didn't even make sense to her. "I don't understand."

"I vouched for you," he said bluntly. "I told them you were mine."

She blinked at the word *mine*, heat flooding through her, heat and shyness and shame. *Mine* was such a possessive word, a word implying ownership, control. It was a word two-year-olds loved, but not one she would have expected to come from a man. At least in the United States you'd never hear a man refer to a woman as his. "How could being… *yours*…free me?"

"By claiming you, I have personally vouched for you."

She was even more confused than before. "Claimed me… how?"

"I said you were my betrothed."

Betrothed? The archaic word didn't make sense for a moment and then it hit her. *"Engaged?"*

Appalled, she saw him nod.

"Because of our…relationship…you are protected for the time being."

Liv's mouth opened but she couldn't make a sound, couldn't think of a single thing to say. Instead shock washed over her in gigantic mind-numbing waves, and before she could think of anything to say, the butler materialized with a tray of small sandwiches, pastries and a large pot of tea. He placed the tray on the low table in the living room and served them both sandwiches, pastries and tea, before departing.

Liv stared at one of the small open-faced sandwiches on her plate. "We're not really engaged," she said at last, finally finding her voice.

"I gave them my word," he said bluntly.

"Yes, but that was to get me out. That was to free me—"

"And I did, but we had complications on the way out of Jabal. Remember that police stop earlier today? They'd come for you. They'd learned that you'd been released from Ozr and they'd been given instructions to seize you. The only way I could protect you was by claiming you. And once I claimed you, they couldn't touch you."

"But you will still send me home, right? You are going to put me on a plane first thing in the morning…." Her voice trailed off as she stared at his face, his expression hard and unyielding.

She tried again. "If you were going to send me home earlier, what has changed?"

"Everything. It has been announced by the Jabal government that we are engaged. They cannot be faulted. It is what I told them, and my honor is based on my word. My word is central to who I am, and to who my family is. I…we Fehrs…do not break our word."

"We're not really going to get married."

"Today at Ozr you said you wanted out, you begged me to get you out, and I did what you asked me to do."

It was just beginning to hit her that she'd celebrated her release from the Ozr prison far too soon.

Her panicked gaze searched the fierce lines of his face, the high brow, the long aquiline nose, the generous but unsmiling mouth, as tremors of fear coursed through her. "There must be another way. There must be some other way...."

He didn't answer and his silence terrified her. "Sheikh Fehr," she pleaded. "Don't tell me we have no other options. I can't believe there aren't any other options."

"There is another option," he said flatly. "And you're right. It's not a done deal yet. You can choose to return to Ozr—"

"To Ozr?" she interrupted, stunned. It'd been hell, sheer hell, locked up there. No sunlight, no bathroom facilities, no running water to speak of. "People die there all the time!"

"It isn't a good place," he agreed.

She bolted up from her chair, nearly upending her plate. "So why would you think I'd want to go back there?"

"Because as of now, those are your only two options. Marriage to me or a return to Jabal."

She sank back down, her legs suddenly impossibly weak. Her gaze clung to his, trying to see, trying to understand if he was absolutely serious. "But you don't want to marry me. There can't be any possible benefit for you!"

His upper lip curled. "None that come to mind."

"So why?"

His features hardened, his dark eyes almost glittering with silent anger. "What would you have me do? Let you rot in prison for the rest of your life? Tell your brother to be glad you're in prison because you're at least not dead?"

She dropped her gaze, her cheeks flaming. Jake would have been desperate, too. He'd always been so protective of her, the quintessential big brother. "You don't have to do this. You didn't ask for any of this—"

"Did you smuggle the drugs?" he demanded harshly, abruptly.

Her head jerked up. *"No."*

His shoulders twisted. "Then I have to do it. If you are innocent, how do I stand by and do nothing? How do I explain to your brother that your life has no value? That his love for you means nothing here? How do I live with myself knowing that all your lives have been laid to waste over someone else's mistake?"

"You're one of those men with a hero complex," she said, feeling desperation hit. "I've read about people like you. Heroes are ordinary people who do extraordinary things—"

"I'm not a hero," he interrupted roughly. "But I did go to Jabal and you are here now, and we've got to get through this."

"But marry…" Her voice faded and she stared at him with disbelief. "It seems so extreme, so…impossible."

His dark head, with his crisp, short black hair inclined. "It's not what you'd choose, or what I'd choose, but it was the only way. Is the only way."

"For *now*," she said.

He said nothing, just stared at her.

She raised her chin, silently defiant. *For now*, she repeated, making a vow to herself that she'd never be forced into marriage, nor marry a man she didn't love.

There was another way out of this. There had to be.

Turning her head away, Liv looked out the window again. The sun was beginning to drop in the sky and long gold rays of light haloed the Great Pyramid.

"Finish your tea," Khalid said, his voice flat, authoritative. "Then we'll go shop. We're entertaining tonight and you'll need proper clothes to impress our distinguished guests."

She reluctantly tore her gaze from the window and glanced back at Khalid. "Who are we entertaining?"

"Friends from Jabal and Egypt who come to celebrate our engagement tonight."

Liv's blood froze, her insides turning to ice. "Jabal officials will be here tonight?"

"You don't need to be afraid," he answered. "They will see you, but they won't speak to you, not without permission from me, and I won't give them permission."

She nodded once.

"But you will have to look happier than that tonight. Tonight's a party, so finish your tea, and then we'll go shopping."

She stared at him in horror. A party tonight to celebrate their engagement? Jabal officials coming here, to their hotel? "I have to pretend we're engaged?"

"Don't worry. I'll see you properly clothed, and I realize you can't shop in your prison-issued robe. Dr. Hassan was kind enough to pick up something from an Egyptian designer we both know. She brought it with her, and it's hanging in the hall closet now. I don't know how well it'll fit, but there's a dress, coat, some undergarments and even a pair of shoes."

"The point isn't the clothes—"

"But it is," he interrupted. "We're having a small party here tonight and you have to be properly attired, so finish your tea and then get dressed as I've arranged to have a stylist meet us in an hour and traffic is going to be ugly."

CHAPTER FOUR

HAVING finished her tea, Liv studied herself in her bedroom mirror. The wheat-colored linen dress and matching coat hung on her slim frame, but the fabric was gorgeous, as was the warm color that reminded her of the pyramid outside.

She'd lost a lot of weight in the past month, her body more angular than attractive. She frowned and combed the brush through her hair, leaving the unruly white-gold strands tumbling loose past her shoulders.

Downstairs in front of the hotel, one of Sheikh Fehr's black Mercedes sedans waited for them. Soon they were driving across Cairo to the First Residence Complex, which is where the luxury shopping mall was also located.

Khalid told her that the First Residence Complex, which included the First Residence Shopping Mall and the Four Seasons Hotel, was the most coveted real estate in Cairo and the place all the stars and sheikhs and heads of state hit when they visit the city.

"But you don't stay there?" she asked, catching glimpses of handsome palm trees lining the broad cornice as the last glints of dying sunlight warmed the creamy paint on the building facades.

"I usually do when I'm here, but on the plane you mentioned your love of history and geography and I thought the Mena House would appeal to you."

"You chose it for me?"

"Yes."

Liv felt that painful tightness in her chest again, and, flustered, she dipped her head, surprised, flattered, but also confused. "Thank you."

The car slowed before an elegant domed building. "We're here," Khalid said, as his driver came around to open the back door. "And I believe your personal shopper is here waiting for us, too."

Indeed, a smart-looking woman in a dark suit stepped toward the car as the driver opened the door. She'd obviously been waiting for them and she bowed deeply to Sheikh Fehr, and gave a smaller bow to Olivia. "I'm Val Bakr," she said, her long dark hair braided and pinned up. "I'm a personal shopper and I'm here to make wardrobing you as quick and efficient as possible."

She led Liv through the shopping center to a selection of designer shops where she'd already selected dozens of outfits for Liv to try on. Khalid accompanied her in each shop, but he sat off to one side and silently observed the fittings.

By the end of the hour Liv had tried on a staggering array of dresses, skirts, slacks, jackets, blouses, gowns, shoes and coats. Raffia totes were added to the pile of clothes, along with small clutches, swimsuits, belts, hats, scarves, and even robes and nightgowns.

The clothes were stunning. Cotton and silk white trousers, off-white patent pumps, a jade-green crocodile belt, a cotton cardigan with real pearl buttons. The rainbow-hued Louis Vuitton bag got its color from pretty leather buttons adhered with a tiny gold ball. The green Valentino heels had a rhinestone bow. The sea-foam green silk chiffon dress had sweet ruffles at the neck and then a high-waisted belt covered in semiprecious stones.

Khalid didn't even hand a credit card. He just nodded at the pile and asked for everything to be sent to him at the Mena Hotel and then he took Olivia's arm and walked her back to his car.

"You can't possibly really buy all that," she said in protest as they exited the elegant shopping mall.

Khalid didn't answer. He just gestured to the car's open door, but Liv hesitated. She could still remember how Val had stood elbow-high in tissue and boxes and garment bags. "Sheikh Fehr, I saw the price on the bag—which alone was seventy-five hundred dollars. I don't even own a *car* worth seventy-five hundred dollars."

Khalid sighed and glanced at his watch. "Miss Bakr has impeccable taste and everything she selected is perfect for our needs."

"But all those clothes! They must cost thousands and thousands of dollars."

"You need a proper wardrobe."

"But this is too much. A couple skirts, a few blouses, a pair of sandals. But certainly not all the designer labels, and those extravagant accessories…and you must admit a seven-thousand-dollar purse—"

"Please get in the car," he interrupted quietly, but in such a no-nonsense tone that Liv gulped a breath and complied.

Inside the car he added, "We do not argue with our women on the city streets, and our women do not disagree with us in front of family, friends or strangers."

Flushing with embarrassment, Liv went hot and then cold and hot again. She was just trying to save him money. She'd only been trying to make things easier. "I'm sorry. I wasn't trying to be disrespectful. I just didn't want you spending so much on me. There was no need."

"But there is," he corrected. "It's what people will expect of you. You now represent me. You are my fiancée, and here in the Arab world, I am very well-known."

"But you must understand I can't pay you back for these things," she protested huskily. "My mom certainly can't. She's nearing retirement, and Jake can't, either. He's a carpenter. He builds houses for a living."

Khalid sighed. "I don't expect to be paid back. But I do expect your respect, and cooperation. I have put my name and reputation on the line for you. I am risking my personal and family honor, and honor is everything here. Honor is the difference between life and death."

It was dark now and the streetlights and building lights illuminated the city blocks.

"My job is to protect you, but you must allow me to protect you. You must trust me when I say we are in a difficult, and dangerous, situation."

Khalid's warning sent a shiver through her. How many times had Jake virtually said the same thing? How many times had he told her the world wasn't a nice place, the world wasn't a safe place, especially for a girl from a small Southern town?

But she hadn't believed him. She'd thought Jake was a pessimist. Now she knew differently.

"Are you listening?" Khalid asked.

"Yes," she answered hoarsely. The things Khalid was telling her terrified her. It wasn't the life she knew. It wasn't how she'd been raised.

"I do not mean to frighten you," he added after a moment, "but I need to impress upon you the importance of appearances. We must be discrete. Everything we do will be observed by others. Everything we do—individually, or together—will be documented, analyzed and discussed. The only time you are truly free, or truly safe, is when you are alone with me."

She gave a short nod to show him she understood.

Khalid fell silent, his forehead creasing, his expression turning brooding. "One more thing. I phoned your brother earlier, while you were finishing your tea. I told him you were safe. I told him you were with me. And I told him you would personally phone later tonight and he said he'd look forward to speaking with you, but in the meantime, he sends love and extends to us his heartiest congratulations."

Liv's blood froze. "Congratulations?" she whispered, through impossibly cold, stiff lips.

"On our engagement."

"You *told* him?"

"I had to. He's going to read it in the paper soon. I thought he'd rather hear the news from us."

"But we're not really going to get married," Liv choked, fingers balling into fists in her lap. "It's just a ruse, a facade to buy us time."

When Khalid didn't answer she felt downright hysterical. He couldn't be serious about marriage. There was just no way. No way. And how was it possible that she'd left prison only to be forced into marriage? Apparently it was just one jail in exchange for another. "I can't do it," she said fiercely, "and I won't."

"Then tell that to the Jabal officials who are coming to see us in an hour or two," he said, doing little to hide his annoyance. "Tell them you're not really my fiancée, tell them it was all a mistake and you'll see what will happen when you get me out of the way. Olivia, I am the only one keeping you from that prison. I am the only one who can, and the only way I can is by offering you my name, my life and my family's reputation."

She hung her head, closed her eyes and dragged in a breath, and then another. "Why does it have to be jail or marriage? Why?"

"Because this isn't Europe, or America, and you were charged with a very serious crime. A crime which can carry the death penalty."

"But why did you have to tell Jake that I was getting married? He didn't have to know. It hasn't happened, and it might not happen—"

"He was going to read it in the papers tomorrow or the next day. I thought he'd want to know first. I thought he'd want to be prepared."

Jake wasn't going to understand, though. Jake knew her. He knew she'd only dated a little and had never had a proper boyfriend. When it came to men she was still ridiculously sheltered and the last thing she'd do, ever, was jump into a relationship with a man she didn't know, much less a man from a culture so very different from hers.

"Jake's just going to be more worried," she said. "It's only going to make things worse."

"It can't be much worse for him that it already is," Khalid answered shortly. "He's had his hands full these past few weeks and the truth is, you are safer with me than you were in Ozr."

"What do you mean, things can't be much worse for him than they already are? What's happened back home?"

Khalid abruptly turned the interior light on, flooding the car with yellow light. "Your mother took the news of your disappearance badly—"

"What do you mean 'badly'? How badly?" she interrupted.

"She had a heart attack—"

"No!" Liv pressed a hand to her mouth. "No," she repeated, voice muffled. "It can't be."

"I understand she's better. She's stable, and resting, but she's still not strong and your brother has been caring for her. Otherwise he'd be here now."

Liv shook her head, her thoughts wild and chaotic. Her entire world had been upended and she couldn't get her bearings. "When did she have the heart attack?"

"A week ago."

With an unsteady finger she reached up to dash away tears before they could fall. "Are you sure she's okay?"

"She's back home. She's sleeping a lot right now."

"That's why you didn't want me to call home earlier."

"Yes."

Exhaling slowly, she drew another painful breath. "I'm not ready to lose my mom. I just lost my dad a couple years ago."

"You must be strong now. You must believe that everything will work out. Everything will be fine."

"Do you really think everything really be fine?"

He gazed down at her for a long, level moment. There was a fierce intelligence in his eyes that reminded her of a hawk or falcon circling before making its kill. "Yes." His long black lashes dropped, concealing his fierce, dark eyes. "It may take time, but things always do work out. One way, or another."

Returning to the hotel, Liv discovered their suite had been transformed. Fresh flower arrangements covered the living room tables while the dining room table had been turned into an elaborate dinner buffet with another huge white-and-purple floral arrangement at the centerpiece.

Soft music played from hidden speakers and a uniformed waiter finished prepping the beverage table, while another moved around the room, fluffing pillows, dimming table lamps and lighting floating candles.

Liv stood in the hall, awed and more than a little bit intimidated by the transformation. In the shimmering candlelight, the faded tapestries on the wall, the dark wood furniture and the rich exotic fabrics covering the couch and chairs seemed almost otherworldly, and Liv realized all over again how far from home she was. How far from anything she knew or understood.

The butler appeared and bowed. "Your attendants are here," he said to Olivia. "They are waiting to help you dress."

Liv shot Khalid a perplexed glance. "My attendants?"

"Miss Bakr thought you might feel more confident tonight if you had help preparing for the party. She sent her favorite stylists. One to do your hair, and the other to…to…" His voice faded and for a moment he looked nearly as perplexed as Liv. "I actually don't know what she's for, but Miss Bakr insisted you have her."

Not entirely reassured, Liv slowly entered her bedroom, not sure what she'd find. Two Egyptian women waited for her. They'd been deep in conversation when Liv arrived but they broke off abruptly to greet her.

"We don't have much time," the hairdresser said briskly, steering Liv straight into the bathroom, where she'd already laid out hair appliances on the marble counter. The curling iron, flat iron and hot rollers were all plugged in, heating, while the blow dryer lay close by, along with a half-dozen bottles of lotion, pomade and hair spray.

"Simple," the other woman said, taking one of Liv's hands in her own to examine her nails. "Tonight it is all about you. Simple. Beautiful. Elegant."

"A goddess," the hairdresser added. "Tonight, you shall be a goddess."

The hairdresser urged Liv to sit down on the chair they'd pulled into the bathroom and while she turned her attention to Liv's clean but tousled blond hair, the other one started in on a pampering manicure.

While they worked she snacked on fruit and cheese and crackers Khalid had sent to her. A glass of champagne also arrived but she didn't dare touch it. She hadn't eaten much in days and feared the alcohol would go straight to her head. However, the assorted cheeses, sweet apricots, grapes and savory flatbreads were delicious and Liv ate virtually everything on her plate.

By the time her hair and nails were finished, Liv felt unusually relaxed and ridiculously spoiled. To have not one, but two, women fuss over her while she snacked on cheese and crackers struck her as incredibly decadent, but she wasn't in a position to argue. Tonight was important. Khalid had made that very clear and she was going to do everything in her power to make a good impression on the visiting officials.

"And your clothes have now arrived," the manicurist said. "We'll just get you into your dress, make sure everything fits exactly so and then leave you to your party."

Her party.

The suggestion was laughable but Liv didn't laugh. She shivered, suffering from a sudden fit of nerves.

She was scared. Nothing could go wrong tonight. She couldn't—wouldn't—go back to Ozr.

Fortunately her attention was drawn to getting dressed. She was to wear a beautiful ivory-pleated gown, the ivory shimmering with threads of gold. A gold collar encircled her throat, the collar the width of her hand and heavy with gold and jewels. The dress was long, touching the tips of her champagne-colored high heels.

The hairstylist had curled her hair in loose waves, and then pinned strategic pieces up so that her hair looked like a golden waterfall with loose tendrils around her face. The manicurist wasn't to be outdone. She swiftly applied a deft application of makeup, including sooty eyeliner, a swirl of black mascara and a soft golden blush on Liv's cheeks, and a touch of golden gloss on her lips.

"You look perfect," the manicurist said, stepping back to examine her handiwork. "So fresh and young and charming, just the way a princess should."

Liv smiled gratefully even as she heard the door open and close. From the sound of voices she knew that the guests had arrived and her smile disappeared as her stomach flipped…a maddening somersault that had her clutching the sink.

"It's going to be fine," the hairstylist said, patting Liv on the back even as Liv leaned over the sink, trying to catch her breath and calm her queasy stomach. "Everything is fine, and you are going to make His Highness very proud. Now go. Enjoy your party."

Her party. A party where she had to pretend she was engaged to Prince Khalid Fehr, Sheikh of the Great Sarq Desert. How could she do it? She was just a girl from Pierceville, a girl who'd never had more than twelve dates in her entire life.

Her stomach rose up again in protest. She couldn't do it, couldn't go out there, not if the Jabal secretary of security was here….

But then she thought of her mother, and Jake, and the sheikh himself. They were all counting on her, depending on her to be strong.

And she could be strong. She would be.

Khalid watched Olivia enter the room, the long, loose pleated ivory and gold gown emphasizing her slender frame and delicate beauty. With her head up, her shimmery blond hair slid along her bare shoulders, the curls long and loose like the pleats in her dress.

She'd been pretty in her passport photo and troubling in prison, but entering the room she was simply stunning and Khalid watched her, by turns surprised, proud, hungry, possessive.

The gold arm rings on her slim biceps hid the bruises on her upper arms. Her fair hair, curled and twisted back from her face, revealed her elegant features, her pale, flawless complexion and her astonishing goddesslike composure.

He knew she didn't want to be here tonight, knew she'd been terrified to face the secretary of security from Jabal, but one wouldn't know it looking at her. Her expression was serene, her blue gaze focused, intelligent, poised.

Beautiful, he thought, she was beautiful and so small and fragile and not of this world.

And she was his.

His.

Khalid's body grew hot, tight, his chest constricting with emotions he didn't know he could feel.

He wanted her, and he'd protect her. Forever.

"She doesn't wear a head-covering or robe," the Jabal official said under his breath, turning an accusing eye to Khalid.

"She doesn't have to," Khalid answered evenly. "She's here with me."

"But you parade her like a—"

"Careful," Khalid interrupted. "She is my future bride, and

I have vowed to protect her with my life. I will not allow anyone to insult her."

The secretary of security clamped his jaw together, his nostrils flaring, and for a moment he couldn't speak and then he choked, "If she really is your betrothed, when is this wedding going to take place? Because it is unlawful for an unmarried man and woman to be together like this, unchaperoned—"

"But she is chaperoned. Her attendants are in her room now." The corner of Khalid's mouth lifted sardonically. "Perhaps you'd like to meet her attendants personally, Mr. Al-Awar?"

One of the Egyptian dignitaries interjected. "That is not necessary, Your Highness, your word is good enough for us, and may I extend our warmest congratulations on your coming nuptials?"

"Thank you," Khalid answered, keeping an eye on Olivia as she stood at the far end of the living room. She looked very small and vulnerable standing on her own and he found himself wishing his brother Sharif was here tonight with his American wife, Jesslyn. Although Jesslyn was now the Queen of Sarq, she was a former schoolteacher and one of the kindest, most genuine women Khalid had ever met. Jesslyn was just the sort of woman Olivia needed in her corner right now.

"When are these nuptials?" the Jabal official pressed. "I haven't heard a date mentioned, which troubles me, and my government. If your engagement is just a hoax—"

"If you've come to insult me, then perhaps it's best if you go now before I take personal offense." Khalid fixed his attention completely on the secretary of security.

"The paperwork stated she was a family member."

"And she is." Khalid's upper lip curled.

"So there will be a wedding."

"Royal weddings take time and my family is scattered at the moment. Once we can bring us all together on a mutually agreeable date, the ceremony will take place."

The Jabal official was silent a long moment before awkwardly nodding his head. "Very good. And congratulations again."

"Thank you." Khalid smiled, showing a hint of his teeth. "And now I shall join my fiancée, but I do hope you'll stay and enjoy our hospitality. The hotel chef has outdone himself and there is much to sample." With a nod he left the men and headed to Olivia.

Olivia watched Khalid walk toward her. While she'd dressed, he'd also changed, donning the traditional Arab robeing.

"Enjoying the party?" he asked on reaching her side.

She nearly smiled at his ironic tone. "It's not much of a party."

His warm gaze slowly swept over her, resting indulgently on her upturned face, lingering even longer on her lips. "I promise that one day we'll throw you a proper party, one with lots of interesting people."

"As long as there's no one from the Jabal government there, I'll be happy."

He glanced toward the dignitaries now crowding around the buffet, piling their plates with food. "I'd tend to agree with you there."

Before she could respond he turned back to look at her. "You look beautiful tonight. Like a goddess." His dark gaze met hers and held. "And I don't give compliments often. I also never say what I don't mean."

Liv's insides felt funny, and her chest grew tight as though she'd swallowed an air bubble, but she knew it was nerves, and this odd emotion he stirred in her. This morning she'd thought it was fear. Now she wasn't so sure. "Thank you. I'm glad you approve."

By the time Liv went to bed an hour and a half later, she was so exhausted she was asleep the moment her head touched the pillow.

In his room, Khalid didn't find it so easy to fall asleep. Usually when he closed his eyes he found absolute silence, and darkness, a stillness that wrapped him completely, blanketing thought, emotions, need. But tonight when he closed his eyes he saw eyes, blue eyes, eyes with long sooty lashes, eyes that were too big in a face that was too small and pale.

But he didn't want to be thinking of Olivia, didn't want to become emotionally involved—or attached—in any way.

He hadn't left his desert and isolation to become entangled in a relationship. He liked being a bachelor, enjoyed his life as a loner, and yet suddenly marriage seemed like a very real, and very constraining, possibility.

And he was the one who'd vowed to never marry.

Khalid passed a hand over his face, trying to erase the picture of Olivia from his mind, trying to create the desert's stillness, but he couldn't shake Olivia's blue eyes, couldn't erase her shock and fear from his mind's eye.

He was still lying awake hours later when he heard her scream. It was a piercing scream and Khalid was on his feet immediately, bursting through the door separating the two bedrooms in the royal suite to flick on the light.

But once in Olivia's room he discovered she was still asleep.

Standing motionless in her doorway, he watched her sleep, wondering what it was that had made her cry out, and hesitating in case she called out again. But minutes passed and she didn't cry again. Instead she slept on, her long blond hair spilling across the pillow, her left hand curled beneath her cheek and chin.

Sleeping, all the worry and pain disappeared from her face. Sleeping, she reminded him of a young girl with all her hopes and dreams still before her.

He'd just turned out the light and was closing the door, turning to leave, when Olivia's voice reached him.

"'Night, Jake," she said sleepily, her voice soft in the darkness.

Jake. The big brother.

His jaw suddenly flexed, tension and pain rippling through him. He'd once been the big brother, too, to younger sisters, too.

But they'd died over ten years ago. They'd died and there was absolutely nothing he could do for them.

Maybe that's why he was here, risking life and limb for Olivia. She was someone's little sister.

"Good night, Olivia," he said quietly, closing the door behind him, and as the door shut, he realized why he couldn't sleep earlier.

Olivia was waking him up. Making him feel again. And feeling emotions *hurt*.

Feeling was the last thing he wanted to do.

CHAPTER FIVE

KHALID was woken by the sound of his phone ringing. Groaning as it continued to ring, he reached out and grabbed the small wireless phone from the table beside his bed.

He recognized the number immediately. His eldest brother, Sharif.

Answering, he rolled over onto his back. "You're a king and a newlywed," Khalid said, his deep voice husky with sleep. "What are you doing calling so early?"

"You promised me you wouldn't break any laws."

Khalid rolled his eyes. "I didn't."

"The president of Jabal wants her back."

"He's not the president, he's a dictator, and the Red Cross and United Nations are both extremely concerned by his regime's disregard for human life."

"Khalid, this is serious."

"I know it is," Khalid answered mildly, but both of them knew that Khalid was the Fehr brother least likely to compromise. "And Olivia's not going back. Not now, not ever."

Sharif sighed heavily. "You freed her by illegal means."

"I rescued her from Ozr, which is synonymous with hell and you know it."

"You claimed her. You claimed her as your fiancée."

"Yes, I did."

"That's a lie—"

"Not if I marry her." Khalid nearly smiled at Sharif's sharp intake.

"That's ridiculous," Sharif protested tersely. "You've spent the past ten years making it clear that you're not interested in people, or relationships or emotions. You've pushed everyone close to you away. You don't even return phone calls—"

"She's in trouble."

"The world's in trouble, Khalid. That doesn't mean you can save everyone."

"I'm not trying to save everyone."

"No?"

"No."

Sharif muttered something unintelligible before adding, "They believe your Miss Morse is part of a huge drug ring."

"She's not," Khalid answered flatly.

"But what if she is?"

Khalid fell silent. He'd considered the very same point. What if Olivia wasn't innocent? What if she was part of this drug smuggling ring? What if the others were just better at the game and she was the one who got caught?

What if there weren't any others involved?

What if she'd lied to everyone about everything?

"I've run a background check on her," he answered after a moment. "There is nothing in her past that indicates she has the experience, or worldliness, to pull something like this off. She lives in the middle of nowhere—a small town in the south—and it's a genuine small town, population thirteen thousand."

"Just the kind of girl to crave fame and fortune."

"Her mom's a homemaker, her older brother is a carpenter and builds houses."

"Khalid," Sharif said, a caution in his voice. "You can't mean to marry her—"

"Why not? You married a schoolteacher. I can marry a travel agent."

"Not funny. I knew Jesslyn for years. She was best friends with our sisters. Furthermore, she wasn't a criminal."

Khalid, uncomfortable with the mention of Aman and Jamila, rolled into a sitting position, naked save for the sheet partially covering his lap. "I won't marry a criminal."

"Not even to save her. Because I know you. You have this thing about rescuing broken creatures, but marriage is different. You can't damage your name—our name—for someone like that. It's not fair to my children, or our brother—"

"I know," Khalid interrupted, smothering his irritation. Sharif had always played the heavy. It was a role he seemed to relish. "I've a week to uncover the truth, and I promise you, I intend to do everything I can to uncover the truth."

"What if a week isn't enough, brother?"

Khalid ran his hand through his short hair, trying to comb it flat. "Then we're all in trouble."

Hanging up, Khalid stepped into a loose pair of cotton pajamas and walked to the balcony, where he drew the curtains open, revealing the pyramid bathed in pink morning light.

One week, he thought. One week wasn't long. He had a lot to do in seven days, a lot to learn, and the best way to learn was to observe.

He needed to get Olivia alone, away from the crowds and noise and distractions of Cairo. He needed to find out just what happened that day she was arrested. He also wanted to find the group she'd been traveling with, including the elusive Elsie, who'd allegedly given the drugs to Liv to carry.

So the first order of the day's business was to ensure Liv had phoned home last night as she'd promised she would before she went to bed.

The second was to make their engagement official—which included putting a ring on Liv's finger.

And the last was to learn more about this fiancée of his, and the best way to do it was to leave urban Cairo behind for the old Egypt, the one of pharaohs, temples and archaeological digs.

Liv was already awake and dressed in a pretty blue-and-white seersucker sundress when Khalid appeared. She'd been sitting in the living room having coffee and flipping through one of the many newspapers the butler had presented her earlier.

"It's everywhere," she said, looking up when Khalid entered the room. "It's in every paper, on the front page, and again inside other sections. Your engagement is front page news."

"Our engagement," he corrected evenly, reaching for one of the papers off the table. He was dressed very casually in a European wardrobe of dark slacks and a long-sleeved white shirt with the cuffs folded back.

"When does this end?" she choked, sitting up taller. "How does it end?"

"It doesn't. We're in this together. For better or worse," Khalid said, shooting her a hard, narrowed look. He'd just showered and his hair was still damp, his jaw freshly shaven. "It could be worse, too. You could still be in Ozr."

She just looked at him, her stomach a bundle of nerves. Perhaps he didn't find the idea of a marriage of convenience intolerable, but she did. She wanted to love the man she married. She wanted to be wooed and won, swept off her feet, and fall head over heels in love.

She wanted a proper wedding, too, but then, didn't every girl? Over the years Liv had imagined her wedding in detail, from the white silk dress to the pale pink floral swags in the white steepled church.

"I'm not marrying a man I don't love," she said almost fiercely, her cheeks burning. "And when I do meet him, Sheikh Fehr, I'm not getting married without my mother attending."

"I appreciate your romantic sentiments," he answered,

dropping one paper and reaching for another. "I do. And as a man who had two younger sisters, I understand how important romance is for you women. But romance isn't practical. And romance isn't going to save you so I suggest letting go of the fairy tale to focus on reality. By the way," he continued, "how did you sleep last night?"

"Well enough, I suppose," she answered hesitantly. "Why?"

"No bad dreams?" he persisted.

She frowned at him, trying to remember if anything had disturbed her sleep. "I don't think so."

"All right. Good. And you do look better today. You still have those shadows under your eyes, but at least you've got some pink in your cheeks. Yesterday you were very pale."

"I was exhausted," she admitted.

"Were you able to call your family before you went to bed?"

She nodded, recalling the brief five-minute conversation. Her mom and brother were on the phone at the same time and her mother still found it difficult to speak for too long without getting winded, so Liv and Jake did most of the talking, but even then, they were both quite careful to say nothing that would upset their mother.

"It was fine," she said. "I was tired and not as talkative as I could be. But at least they know I'm safe, and, well…and they don't have to worry anymore." She hesitated. "I was surprised, though, that Jake didn't mention your call to him, but maybe he didn't feel right talking about it with Mom on the phone."

"I imagine he's doing his best to protect your mom." The edge of his mouth curved. "It's what men want to do for their women, whether it's their wife or their mother."

Intrigued by this revelation, she probed for more information. "Are you close with your mother?"

"No," he answered, and instead of elaborating glanced at his watch. "Feel like shopping?"

Liv wrinkled her nose. "Not particularly."

"You don't enjoy shopping?"

"We shopped yesterday."

He looked at her strangely, deep grooves forming on either side of his full mouth, his upper lip slightly bowed, but not quite as full as his sensual lower lip. For the first time she noticed he had a hint of a cleft in his chin. Definitely handsome, if not completely overwhelming.

"Women love to shop," he said.

"I don't, unless I'm buying travel books or history books or something that I can read." She watched his face, trying to gauge his reaction, but his expression was perfectly blank. "I was actually hoping we could go sightseeing." She hesitated. "See the pyramids or visit the Sphinx."

Before Khalid could answer, the suite's doorbell chimed and the butler emerged from a back room to go to the door. Liv could hear the door open, and then listened as he greeted someone and then the door closed again. The butler entered the living room with an older Egyptian in a dark suit following close at his heels, a large leather briefcase in one hand.

"Your Highness," the older Egyptian said, greeting Khalid with a deep bow. "I hope I didn't keep you waiting."

"Not at all," Khalid answered. "We were just discussing the day."

The man bowed again. "Is there someplace in mind you'd like to do this? Shall I join you there in the sitting area, or would you prefer to move to the dining room?"

Khalid glanced at Liv where she sat, and then into the dark dining room. "I think the light is better here," he answered, "and Olivia is already comfortable. Let's just do this where we are."

"Excellent." The man carried his briefcase to the low coffee table between the upholstered pieces of furniture and set his briefcase down. It wasn't until he placed the briefcase on the table that she noticed it was handcuffed to his wrist.

Shocked, she watched him take a tiny key from another

pocket and undo the clasp on the handcuff, before turning his attention to the locked briefcase.

Glancing at Khalid, she realized he wasn't at all surprised by the elaborate security measures. Then when the man opened the briefcase, she understood why.

It was filled with diamond rings. Rows and rows of diamond rings in the velvet-covered, foam-lined briefcase. There had to be at least twenty rings, maybe thirty, and the diamonds were enormous. They started in the three- or four-carat range and went all the way to three or four times that size.

But not all the diamonds were the traditional clear stone. Parts of the rows glittered with pastel light, and a dozen rings featured the incredibly rare and costly pink and yellow diamonds.

Each diamond was cut differently, too, and the shapes and styles dazzled her—marquise cut, emerald cut, oval, pear. The settings were all unique, too, with prongs inset with diamonds, the bezels paved, every setting glittering with fire and light.

"I know you said you don't enjoy shopping, but I do think you should pick the ring you'll wear," Khalid said.

"It's not just a ring," the Egyptian jeweler said soberly, "it's a symbol of your commitment, and you'll want a ring that will always remind you of your love and vows—"

"Khalid," Liv murmured, rising to her feet. "May I please have a word with you?"

"Of course," he answered, "but we can speak freely here. Mr. Murai is an old friend of my family's and has been in the jewelry business a long time. You are not the first jittery bride-to-be he has helped."

Liv's frustration grew. Khalid was deliberately misunderstanding her. "I'm just overwhelmed," she said. "I don't think I can make this decision today. Perhaps at the end of the week…?"

"I want my ring on your finger," Khalid answered bluntly. "It's important to me. It's important to my people, and it's important to my family."

"But I don't know anything about diamonds or jewels—"

"Which is why Mr. Murai is here. He's not just the best in Cairo, he's one of the best jewelers in the world. Most of the royal families use him."

But she didn't want to wear a ring, especially not a ring like this. None of these was just a simple band, but a statement of wealth, a statement of style and lifestyle—all things Liv wasn't comfortable with.

"I understand you want me to wear a ring," she said, swallowing with difficulty, "but these rings are too much. They're so elaborate, and large and more than I need."

"Miss Morse, I understand this can be overwhelming," Mr. Murai said kindly. "Selecting one's ring is often a very emotional decision and it requires time and thought. Please, won't you sit down again and tell me a little about what you'd like? There's no hurry, no pressure. We shall take as much time as you need, we will try every ring, and if nothing pleases you, I shall go, search out more beautiful choices and bring them back to you."

Liv looked up at Khalid as the jeweler spoke and she stared at him hard, wanting to tell him that she still wasn't happy even as she knew that Khalid would have his way.

She couldn't fight with Khalid in front of the jeweler. Khalid had said appearances mattered. He said everything they did would be scrutinized, including her wardrobe, her jewelry, and what she wore—or didn't wear—on her ring finger.

Slowly she sat back down on the couch. "I don't know very much about diamonds," she said, her voice pitched low.

"That's fine, I can teach you what I know."

She nodded, aware of Khalid standing behind the jeweler, aware that he'd hardly glanced at the case of jewels. Instead his entire focus seemed to rest on her.

"Do you have any favorite pieces at home?" the jeweler persisted.

She blushed shyly. "I don't own very much jewelry, just an opal ring my brother's former girlfriend brought me back from Australia, and a pearl necklace my father gave me when I turned eighteen."

"No diamonds?" the jeweler asked.

"No diamonds."

"Well, then, we will make sure your first is exactly right for you." Mr. Murai gestured to the front row of diamonds. "I don't know if diamonds are truly a girl's best friend, but I do know diamonds are timeless. The popularity of the cut might come and go, but the stone itself remains the most popular of all gemstones.

"There are three very popular cuts at the moment," he continued. "The marquise, rose and cushion. All the rings in this front row are one of those cuts. As you can see," he said, lifting one of the rings and tilting it to catch the light, "the marquise cut is boat-shaped, pointed at both ends and one of the most popular cuts today although it dates back to the 1700s."

She watched him tip the ring this way and that, amazed at how the ring glowed all the way through, glinting with bits of fire and light. "It's very pretty."

He glanced up at her. "But not right for you?"

"It's very dramatic," she answered.

Smiling, Mr. Murai replaced the large marquise cut diamond ring and picked up another. "This is a rose cut, and the rose cut was developed in the sixteenth century. As you can see, it's a very glamorous, very elegant look. Some people think it's classic Hollywood, others see it and think of the crown jewels. You'll notice there's a flat base and all the facets radiate from the center."

It was beautiful, but not her. The setting was beautiful, too, but it just felt too…old, too much like what a grandmother might wear. Not that her grandmother had ever owned a diamond bigger than a half carat.

"Not for you," the jeweler guessed, slipping the ring back

and reaching for another. "This one dates to the 1600s and it's known as the cushion cut. Note the square or rectangular shape and the rounded corners. Many people think a diamond's brilliance is particularly enhanced by this cut."

"That's gorgeous, too," she said, but there was no way she'd ever wear a ring that big, or a stone that large. "How big a carat is that?" she asked, just out of curiosity.

"Just under twelve carats."

"Heavens," she choked, recoiling. "Twelve carats? Who could afford that?"

"Your fiancé," Mr. Murai answered evenly, putting the ring back. "His brothers. Their friends."

"I'm sorry, but I find it almost offensive—" She broke off apologetically. "I just couldn't in good conscience ever wear something like that when I know half the world is starving. It doesn't seem right."

Khalid abruptly moved forward, leaned over the open briefcase and searched the trays of rings. "That one," he said, pointing to a two-and-a-half-carat yellow pear-shaped diamond in a platinum band. Smaller diamonds sparkled at the prongs.

Mr. Murai took the ring out of the case. "One of my favorite rings," the jeweler said, twisting it to capture the light. "Very classic, and very, very elegant."

It was beyond beautiful, and it wasn't something she would have ever chosen to try, but there was something in the shape and the design that captured her imagination.

"Try it on," the jeweler encouraged.

Uncertainly Liv slid the ring onto her left hand and gazed down at the flawless diamond, the palest yellow. The ring made her skin look creamy, while the stone itself reminded her of sun and sweet, ripe fruit and lemon meringue.

She turned her hand to the light, then dropped her hand low and finally brought the ring up near her face to inspect the exquisite setting more closely.

"It suits you," Khalid said quietly.

She looked up at him, her cheeks flushed. "It's the most beautiful ring I've ever seen."

"Is there anything else you'd like better?" he asked.

"No," she answered breathlessly, curling her fingers, feeling the weight of the stone against the back of her finger and the smooth warm fit of the platinum band on her skin. "But it's too much, far too much—"

"That is the ring," Khalid said, turning to Mr. Murai. "Can we have it sized this morning and returned to us before our noon flight?"

Mr. Murai nodded. "Not a problem."

"We'll leave for the airport at eleven-thirty," Khalid added.

Liv looked at him, and then back at the ring, which was still enormous at two and a half carats, and yet it was also beautiful, beyond beautiful, and she couldn't believe it was going to be hers.

It shouldn't be hers. She wasn't really going to marry Khalid. She was going to go home and get back to her job and become just Liv Morse again, but until then, would it be so awful to actually wear something this lovely? God knows, she'd never have anything like this again.

Girls like her didn't own jewels. Girls like her just admired them in magazines.

"I'll have the ring sized immediately," the jeweler answered, "and will personally bring it back to you."

After Mr. Murai left with his briefcase of rings, Liv stood at the window with the view of the Great Pyramid, feeling increasingly pensive.

She shouldn't have said yes to the ring. It wasn't proper. Nice girls—*good girls*—didn't accept expensive gifts from men, much less from men like sheikhs and desert princes.

Her mother would have another heart attack if she knew Liv was even wearing a ring like that.

"It's just a ring," Khalid said flatly, standing not far behind her. "You haven't damned your soul yet."

She glanced at him over her shoulder. *"Yet."*

His generous mouth with that slightly bowed upper lip curved in amusement. "Most women love trinkets."

"Sheikh Fehr, yellow diamonds aren't trinkets."

"I don't think you can continue with the Sheikh Fehr title now that we're engaged."

"But we're not really engaged."

His faint smile disappeared, and his chiseled features grew harder, fiercer. "On the contrary, we really are, and in just a few hours you'll have the ring to prove it."

CHAPTER SIX

MR. MURAI returned to the hotel by eleven with the sized ring and by eleven-thirty she and Khalid were in the car, heading for the airport.

At Cairo's executive airport they boarded the royal jet for Aswan, the southernmost outpost of ancient Egypt, a city five hundred and fifty miles south of Cairo.

During the first half hour of the flight, Khalid stared out the window, reflecting on the early morning phone call from his brother.

Sharif had been wrong about several things, but he had been right when he said that Khalid had pushed people away and severed relationships. Khalid didn't want anyone dependent on him, much less emotionally dependent. He needed space—freedom—and he wasn't ready to give it up.

He'd do what he had to do to get Olivia home, but this wasn't about love. It wasn't about emotion. It was duty. Pure and simple.

The flight attendant appeared to tell them she would soon be serving lunch, and proceeded to set up a table that locked into the floor in between their club chairs, turning the sitting area into a cozy dining room.

Liv glanced at Khalid as the flight attendant spread a pale gold linen cloth over the table. She didn't want to be intimidated by him but there was something overwhelming about him. She didn't know if it was his silence, or the stillness in his powerful frame, but he reminded her of the desert he lived in. Remote, detached, aloof. A desert—and a man—she wanted nothing to do with.

Horrifying tears suddenly started to her eyes. She reached up and knocked them away with a knuckle. She hadn't cried in Ozr. She certainly wasn't going to cry now, but she'd gotten her hopes up. She'd thought—imagined—she was free. She'd thought that once she left Jabal with Khalid she was just one step away from home. But instead of home, they were setting off on a different journey. A new journey. A journey she wasn't ready, or willing, to take.

The flight attendant served their first course, sizzling prawns, on the Fehr royal china, with its distinctive geometric gold-and-black pattern that struck Liv as exceptionally Egyptian.

Baked red snapper in a lightly spiced tomato sauce followed the sizzling prawns, with a minted pomegranate yogurt on sliced grapefruit presented for dessert.

They ate with almost no conversation or discussion, which did little to ease Liv's nerves. "We don't eat like this on commercial air flights," she said awkwardly as the last of the dishes were cleared away. "Especially not in economy." She took a quick breath, adding in a rush, "Not that you'd ever fly economy."

His brow lowered. "I'm sure I have once."

She waited a good minute, and Khalid was still thinking. "You haven't," she answered for him, "or you'd remember. It's horrendous, especially on international flights when you have to sleep sitting up and you can't because you've been cramped for so long.

"There's no room for your tray table," she added, "no room to lean back, no place for your legs or feet, and the people sitting on either side of your seat hog the armrests, which squishes you even more."

He grimaced. "I'd never fly if I had to fly like that."

"I actually didn't think it was going to be so bad. I sell coach tickets all the time but it was miserable. I just kept thinking once I arrived in Morocco the trip would get better…." Her voice faded and she stared out the window at the impossibly blue sky.

After a moment she drew a deep breath and looked back at Khalid. "I honestly don't know how everything went so wrong. I thought I was being careful. Cautious. I avoided going out on my own, didn't dress provocatively, never allowed myself to be alone with men…" Her voice drifted off as she shook her head. "I'm just so disappointed. Not just with the world, but with me."

"Why are you disappointed with yourself?"

"I thought I was smarter. Better prepared. I thought I could take care of myself and instead I end up arrested and in prison." She clasped her hands in her lap. "But it's my fault I ended up there. I have no one else to blame but me."

"And how is it your fault?"

Liv struggled to explain it, but the words didn't come. How could she make him understand exactly what had happened that day? It was already such a blur. Just remembering the day she was arrested filled her with cold, icy despair. She bit into her lower lip as she searched for the right words.

"I offered to hold Elsie's bag," she said at last, her voice unsteady. "I had a backpack and she had that awkward purse. I told her to slip her purse in my backpack so she wouldn't lose it."

Khalid listened intently. "Did you know Elsie well?"

Liv shook her head. "No, we'd only met a couple days earlier. She was part of this big group of people in their twenties from Europe, the U.S. and Australia. There were guys, girls, a very friendly international crowd. A lot of them had met while traveling through Spain, and then they crossed from the tip of Spain into Morocco, and that's where I met them. We traveled around Morocco for a week before deciding we'd go to Jabal."

"Why Jabal?"

"We missed the bus to Cairo and it seemed like an adventure. No one really goes to Jabal anymore, and yet everyone heard it was cheap and we could catch a bus to Cairo from Jabal's capital."

"That was the destination—Egypt?"

"We all wanted to see the pyramids and the tombs. That's why I ended up joining them in the first place. I was trying to be smart, proactive. I thought I'd be safer traveling with a group of people than being on my own—" She broke off, realizing all over again how wrong she'd been, and the shock of it, and the anger over it, surged through her, wild, fierce, uncontrollable.

"If you hadn't come…" she said, her voice muffled. "If you hadn't come I would have never gotten out."

"But I did come, and I've promised you my continued protection."

She lifted her head to look at him and her eyes met his and held. His eyes were so dark, so commanding, that she couldn't look away, and Liv didn't know if it was the heat there in his eyes, or his slightly rough rumble of a voice, but shivers raced through her, shivers of hope and fear, anticipation and curiosity.

He was so very much a man—confident, controlled, a little ironic, a little intimate. The combination was incredibly dangerous, especially for someone like her who had such limited experience with men.

With the table now collapsed and once again stowed, she found she'd missed the protection it offered.

The table had created a sense of distance and space, and with it gone, Khalid seemed even more imposing than before. He was sitting close, very close, not even an arm's length away, and even though they weren't touching she could feel him, feel his warmth and energy, and it was an electric awareness. Hot, sharp, dizzying.

Liv needed that table back, needed a barrier between them, because right now she felt very exposed, and vulnerable.

Maybe this is why women in the Middle East and Northern Africa hide beneath robes. Maybe they're not hiding their bodies from men, but from themselves.

Interesting how a man could change so much so fast. Liv had never felt delicate before, nor all that feminine, but Khalid made her aware of the differences between them, made her aware that he was bigger, taller, stronger.

He was tall and broad-shouldered and powerfully built. She was smaller, not even reaching his shoulder, and slender. But it was more than height. It was the way they were shaped. The way *she* was shaped. Her narrower shoulders. The swell of her breasts. The curve of her hip. The line of her thigh.

Her wardrobe only accented the differences between them, too. Everything he'd bought for her yesterday was feminine, each piece fresh, charming, stylish and of course perfectly made. Even her blue-and-white seersucker sundress, topped by a small white cardigan edged in lace, emphasized her delicate frame. The 1950s retro-style dress was innocent and yet flirtatious. The bodice molded to her breasts, nipped at her waist and then flared at her hips in a swingy skirt that hit just above her knees.

She shifted, increasingly fidgety, trying not to be aware of the bare skin of her legs, or the rub of the cotton fabric against her breasts. She didn't want to dwell on the parts of her that were covered, and the parts that weren't. Didn't want to think of how warm she was or how strange her body was feeling—tingly, antsy, unsettled.

Khalid had scooped her from Ozr, plucking her from a prison hell only to transform her into a virtual princess overnight. Frankly, it was a bit too Cinderella for her tastes and she didn't trust it. *Any* of it.

"Tell me about where we're going and what we're going to see," she said, trying to distract herself.

"We've left urban Cairo for old Egypt," he said, rising to pull a thick atlas out of one of the cabinets inlaid with exotic wood. "The Egypt of pharaohs and temples and archaeological digs."

"Now you're just torturing me," she answered, thinking he knew all the right things to fire her imagination. "Cairo wasn't on my must-see list of places to go. I wanted the old Egypt with its history and romance. Alexandria, Luxor, Aswan…"

"We'll be visiting Aswan today. Visiting two of those places. We're starting with Aswan and will end up in Luxor. Here, let me show you our stops on the map."

With the atlas opened to an enormous map of Northern Africa, Khalid showed her the border his country shared with Egypt. "You can see we're not far from southern Egypt, and Aswan is the southernmost city in Egypt. You can see why at one point Aswan was viewed as the Siberia of the Roman Empire. No one wanted to go through. It was a long way from Memphis, but Aswan's role in Egyptian history is significant. Those that ruled Aswan were responsible for patrolling the river, for keeping the border of Egypt safe."

Liv was listening, she really was, but as Khalid talked he found it hard to focus on anything except the fact that he was sitting near her, very near, the large atlas open between them. As he talked he drew a line along the Nile River and she found it fascinating to watch the way he used his hands.

He had beautiful hands.

A rather odd realization, she thought, wrinkling her nose, especially as she'd never even noticed men's hands before, but suddenly everything about Khalid was interesting. He was interesting.

She liked the color of his skin, the shape of his fingers, the creases in his knuckles and that tapered index finger as he lightly traced the river and the river valley.

Why was she even looking at his hand? Why was she feeling so edgy? They were just studying a map. He was talking about history. Temples. Monuments, for God's sake.

"Does that sound right?" he asked for a second time and Liv, realizing he was talking to her, jerked her head up and looked into his face, her eyes meeting his.

They were dark eyes, dark brown, so dark she couldn't see anything at all but his eyes. And long black lashes and a faint line between his strong black eyebrows.

"Yes," she said, sounding rather breathless.

The corner of his mouth lifted ever so slightly, and his gaze grew warmer, faint lines at the edge of those mysterious eyes. "Really?"

"Yes," she repeated, wondering why her skin just kept growing hotter and hotter. Her head felt light and her body felt strange.

"You weren't even listening," he flashed, challenging her.

She blushed. He was right. She wasn't listening to a single word he said, too intent on things she'd never noticed before, and emotions she'd never felt. Like a giddy excitement.

And a painful curiosity that burned for something she didn't quite understand yet.

"Okay. I wasn't listening," she confessed, crunching her fingers against her thigh, feeling the sharp press of the diamond, which seemed like nothing compared to the turbulent emotions inside her.

"I thought you were interested in the history."

"I am. I really am."

"But…?"

She could feel heat creep up her neck toward her face. "I don't know. I'm sorry. My mind's just racing. It's really hard for me to focus right now. I think I'm too excited."

His expression eased. "What part overwhelms you the most?"

"Uh, you."

Khalid suddenly grinned, a rare grin of flashing white teeth. The smile was so easy, so wide it reshaped his entire face and for a split second Liv saw a different man, one that had maybe once laughed a great deal, one that had relaxed more, lived more, enjoyed more.

"You're beautiful when you smile," she said, blurting the compliment before she had time to think it through.

His easy smile slowly disappeared, his expression turning speculative again even as they made a sharp turn and dipped, nose tipping for the quick descent. "We're on our way down."

On the ground a convoy of new Range Rovers waited. "More security?" Liv said as they climbed into the four-wheel-drive Range Rover designated for them. Other vehicles were in front, others were behind.

"Always," he answered as the door closed behind him.

"Is everything so dangerous here?"

He glanced at her and his hard features suddenly gentled. "I'm not going to take any risks when it comes to you."

And just like that, he stole her breath, sent her heart racing, her pulse thundering.

Khalid had been imposing in his *dishdashah*, but in his exquisitely tailored Italian suits, he looked so ruggedly handsome that she'd look at him and then moments later, want to look again. No man in Pierceville wore khaki linen suits, and certainly no one managed to look so casual and yet confident at the same time. The lapels of Khalid's jacket hit just so on his broad chest and the cocoa linen shirt was conservatively buttoned with only the top button undone near the collar.

As the car moved forward, she looked at him again, and didn't look away this time. She couldn't. He was just so…

So…

Sexy, she thought, gulping for air.

"There," Khalid said, leaning close to Liv in her window seat to get a better view, "that's Lake Nasser."

She turned to the window. They'd flown over the lake in their final approach, and the dark blue water of the lake had been intensified by the contrast of the desert everywhere else.

"It's enormous," she said, aware of Khalid's shoulder, and knee and thigh.

"It's man-made," he answered. "If we've time we'll visit Aswan Dam, but it's not my favorite place to go."

As he gestured, his broad shoulder brushed against her arm not far from her breast, and a lightning-hot shiver whipped through her. His body had felt warm against hers and hard, too, and just like his hands, she found herself obsessed with his close proximity.

Breathing in, she could smell the heady scent of skin and soap and spice, and it tantalized her, nearly as much as that brush of his shoulder so close to her chest. "You don't sound as though you approve of the dam," she said unsteadily.

Khalid's eyes narrowed. "I have a love-hate relationship with the new lake."

"It's new?"

"The dam was completed in 1971, but the architects of the plan knew a decade earlier that once the dam was complete, some of the world's greatest treasures would be doomed—completely submerged—beneath the huge lake being created behind the new dam."

"Are you serious?"

He nodded grimly. "There was an international outcry, and thankfully my father was one of the first to become involved in the conservation efforts to save these valuable Nubian monuments. From the 1960s until the 1980s he used his own personal resources to help finance the rescue efforts of the Nubian Rescue Campaign. He even participated on one dig where they dismantled the temple stone by stone to have the same temple rebuilt later at Abu Simbel."

Liv didn't know what to say. She suddenly felt very provincial. Her father had never done anything so grand in his entire life. Her father had been a good man, a kind man, but ultimately, he'd been rather simple. "You must be proud of him."

Khalid shifted his shoulders. "I'm proud of every country that participated in the conservation efforts. Archaeologists from Egypt, Sweden, Italy, Germany and France raced to move the massive structures, while other countries also helped underwrite the undertaking. In the end, fourteen monuments were saved—"

"But not all?" she interrupted.

"No. Some disappeared beneath the lake, and I suppose fourteen is better than nothing. Ten of those temples are at Abu Simel—which we'll visit tomorrow—and the other four are in different parts of the world, including one of my favorites, the Temple of Dendur, which has been reconstructed in New York City's Metropolitan Museum of Art."

"Why did four of the temples leave Egypt?"

"The Egyptian government wanted to thank the countries for their significant financial contributions."

"Did Sarq get one?"

"My father wouldn't even consider it. In his mind, the Egyptian monuments belonged in Egypt."

They drove to Shellal where a private boat ferried them to the Isis Temple complex built on Agilika Island. Liv had always been fascinated by stories of Isis, aware that by Roman times, Isis had become one of the greatest Egyptian gods, worshipped everywhere in the Roman Empire, even in distant Britian.

During the ride Liv listened, enthralled, as Khalid told her about old photographs his father had in his library, photographs taken at the turn of the century when Philae was one of Egypt's legendary tourist attractions. "In the early 1900s Philae was a wonder of the Nile. And I can't remember her words exactly, but Amelia Edwards, an Egyptologist, wrote about Philae in her 1877 book, that the island with its palms and colonnades seemed to rise out of the river like a mirage."

"Is Philae one of the places damaged by the dam?"

"Yes. The original Philae Island is now completely submerged, and the temples and artifacts were also submerged for a number of years. People would come out in little rowboats and peer through the water to try to get a glimpse of the sanctuaries lost below."

"I can't imagine all this underwater," she answered, tipping her head back to take in the enormous temple as the boat neared the bank of the island.

"It was a disaster. Horrible. People would row boats out here and try to peer through the water to see the ruins. Thankfully, in 1972 conservationists began to salvage the submerged temple and buildings by constructing a cofferdam around the island and draining the waters. The exposed temple was then disassembled stone by stone, before being transported across the Nile to this place, Agilika Island."

Their boat glided to the base of the Hall of Nectanebo, which Khalid told her was the oldest part of the complex. After stepping out, he assisted her out and together they walked north, through the outer temple court with its long line of colonnades to the entrance of the Temple of Isis itself.

As they explored the island with the various temples and gates and pavilions, Liv felt some of the darkness inside her ease, the sense of doom receding. If she didn't think about the engagement ring on her finger, or the prospect of marriage, she actually felt…happy. Happier than she had in weeks and weeks.

She was seeing ancient Egypt after all. She'd be taking the Nile River cruise she hadn't been able to afford. She'd visit the spectacular monuments on private tours with Sheikh Khalid Fehr, a real desert prince.

She glanced down at the sparkling diamond ring she wore and then bit her lower lip. The engagement, though, still didn't make sense. She loved Egypt. She liked Khalid. But she wasn't marrying him. She couldn't. She didn't even know him. It didn't make sense.

It was late in the afternoon by the time they returned from Philae to their convoy of vehicles. Climbing back in their Range Rover, Khalid told her they were heading to his family's Egyptian sailboat, a boat built for the Nile River, and their home for the next five days.

As they drove Khalid told her that the boat had been built by his father for his family's use but hadn't been completed until a month after his death.

"I think you'll like the boat," he added, "and our captain. He's worked the Nile for nearly forty years and he knows stories about the river that will fascinate you."

The sun was just starting to set when they arrived at the place where the royal sailboat, a magnificent flat-bottomed *dahabieh*, was moored.

For a private sailboat it was large, very large, but not nearly the size of the Greek yachts that sailed the Mediterranean. The *dahabieh* utilized the smart nineteenth-century design but improved on it by ensuring every room and suite was exquisitely furnished and completely comfortable, as well as luxurious.

On the upper deck, an awning covered much of the deck, with striped cotton curtains that could be untied later to shade the deck from the worst of the afternoon sun.

Beneath the top deck, but still above water, were the guest rooms, the living room and the kitchen, as well as the staff quarters.

Khalid's room, the master bedroom, was the largest room, outside the serenely and simply furnished living room. His room, located at the far end of the sailboat, had its own beautiful covered deck, the covered area supported by four hand-painted columns in cream, white and the palest gold.

While sunset painted the sky lavender and red, deckhands went around lighting the large antique lanterns on the upper deck and in the living room.

Liv loved the antique lanterns and the soft flickering light they created, but then everything about the royal *dahabieh* was romantic. Mysterious.

Khalid gave her a brief tour of the boat and then escorted her to her room, the second largest suite.

"We normally eat quite a bit later than you Americans do," he said, glancing around her room to make sure she had her luggage and everything was indeed in order, "but I know it's been a long day and we could eat sooner if you're hungry."

"I am hungry," she admitted. "But if you prefer to wait, I can wait. The last thing I want is to be a demanding guest—"

"You're not a guest anymore. This is your home, too, now. If you're hungry, we eat, and when you're tired, you sleep."

She swallowed hard. "Thank you."

His dark head inclined. "I'll meet you on the upper deck when you're ready. Dinner is usually served there. There's no need to wear anything formal, as we sit at a low table with cushions, but it is a chance to wear something comfortable, that is still a little more special."

"I understand," she answered. But once she'd closed the door she panicked. Not formal. Comfortable. But still special? What was that?

One of the crew had already unpacked her clothes, hanging all the beautiful new skirts and dresses, blouses, slacks and coats in the small closet with her shoes lining the closet floor. The drawers in the painted cabinet on the opposite side of the room were filled with the silk undergarments, stockings, purses and accessories Khalid had insisted on buying.

She flicked through her hanging wardrobe once and then again, finally settling on a chalk-colored cotton cardigan with patent-leather buttons and a nautical, ropelike detail on the sleeves. She'd pair the sweater with white cotton and silk slacks, and a pair of high raffia wedge sandals.

Hair combed and pulled into a low ponytail, face washed and refreshed with lotion and just a little makeup, she climbed the staircase to the upper deck where the lantern flames flickered and danced in the evening breeze.

Less than thirty minutes later they were sitting at a low table at the front of the deck, their table surrounded with pillows and covered in the most gorgeous silk cloth.

They were eating by candlelight, too, their table illuminated by a dozen jeweled candles, the candlelight a perfect complement to the steaming savory pilaf, delicately seasoned lamb, grilled seafood and sautéed vegetables.

It was so peaceful dining on the upper deck. She and Khalid chatted about their afternoon at Philae and compared notes on what each of them had liked best.

Khalid said he appreciated how the new island had been landscaped to resemble the old island as much as possible.

Liv said she loved the stories of Isis, and how devoted she'd been to her husband.

"He was also her brother," Khalid said, tearing a hunk off the bread to mop up the rest of the savory juice on his plate.

"I try not to think about that part," she answered, "because if I do, the story gets a little weird."

Khalid's dark eyes flashed with amusement. "What about the conception of their son, Horus?"

"The part where she reassembles her husband's dismembered body, brings him back from the dead, and um…conceives the baby…and then lets Osiris go back to the underworld? That's weird, too." She leaned back against one of the large pillows. "But it's also kind of cool. She was so devoted to Osiris. She loved him so much. Love like that is rare."

"You're a romantic."

She shrugged and smiled. "I'm a woman."

"And until now, single."

She looked at him, eyebrows half-rising. "Is that a question or a statement?"

"A statement." He shrugged. "Nothing in your background

report indicated you'd ever married, so I assumed you'd remained single." He paused. "You are single?"

Liv sat forward abruptly, no longer as calm or relaxed as she'd been a moment ago. "You had me investigated."

"I have to investigate everyone," he answered unapologetically.

"A hard way to live."

"It's the way I've always lived. The way my family lives." His deep brown gaze met hers and held. "Everyone we meet, everyone we invite here, everyone we spend time with is eventually investigated."

Her skin crawled at the idea of people's lives being examined, researched, investigated and yet he was so casual about it. "Did you discover any dirty, dark secrets in my past?" she demanded hotly. "Anything that shocked you?"

He shook his head, his expression shuttered. "No. You're just as sheltered as I imagined. A babe in the woods."

"You sound disappointed."

"Why would I be disappointed if you aren't experienced?"

Her heart beat faster. Even her palms felt damp. "Were you interested in my life experience, Khalid, or my sexual experience?"

"Are you a virgin, then?"

"I'm sorry. Did the background report leave something out?"

He leaned against his cushions. "Why are you angry?"

"I don't know. Maybe because you had a background check done on me and you know all my juicy little tidbits, but I know nothing about you. You're this big mystery and I'm supposed to be engaged to you."

"You *are* engaged."

She glanced down at the diamond glittering on her ring finger on her left hand. "I *don't* feel like we're engaged. To be honest, I don't feel anything at all."

"Then we have to change that, don't we?"

"How?"

He didn't answer with words. Instead he reached for her, drawing her into his arms and sliding one hand into her hair to cup the back of her neck.

It all happened so fast, so unexpectedly, that she didn't even realize what was happening until his head descended, blotting out the light.

Panicked, Liv stiffened, her mouth opening to protest even as his lips covered hers. His lips slowly moved across hers, coaxing, testing, teasing. She'd never been kissed like this, never kissed with so much control, so much expertise. He made her melt on the inside, made her belly ache and tighten and her lower back tingle over and over again.

Her hands rose to his chest, uncertain if she should push him away or bring him closer, but once her hands settled there, she felt the last of her resistance melt.

He felt good. He felt unlike anything she'd ever felt. His chest was hard, firm, thick with muscle that curved in smooth taut planes, and beneath her palm she could feel the beat of his heart, steady, sure, and somehow that reassured her more than anything else.

She'd never been with a man before, not a man like this. She'd only dated boys and young men, men who hadn't found themselves or their strength, but Khalid was strong, and brave, full of courage and conviction and he wasn't afraid to do what he thought was right....

Wasn't afraid to risk everything to save a woman...

His tongue traced her inner lip the same way his finger had traced the river on the map and she felt like liquid gold in his hands. Kissing Khalid was like kissing the sun; she could feel the desert in his veins, feel his great silent world of endless sand.

He deepened the kiss and she dug her fingers into his shirt. He was making her feel so much and the emotion burned in her, tightening her chest, making her feel hot, hungry, fiery.

When his tongue slipped all the way into her mouth she

trembled from head to toe, her knees clamping together so hard she felt a shock of intense feeling rush through her, a rush that left her dazed by its ferocity.

She wanted something new, something almost wild.

Passion, she thought, as his teeth nipped at her lip, eliciting yet another fierce, hungry response.

She wanted this, him, whatever it was.

His head lifted and his narrowed gaze swept her flushed face. "Tell me, little one," he drawled, his deep voice so husky it sounded hoarse, "do you feel anything yet?"

CHAPTER SEVEN

IN HER bed with moonlight peeking through the slats of the wood shutters, Liv replayed the kiss over and over in her mind.

No one had ever kissed her like that and, putting her fingers to her mouth, she marveled at how sensitive her lips felt now. How sensitive she felt, her body suddenly humming with a brand-new energy. A brand-new awareness.

She'd felt things she didn't even know existed and now the possibilities tantalized her. More energy and more excitement and more of that giddy, dizzying sensation and pleasure.

Lightly she rubbed her fingertips across her mouth, feeling the softness, the swollen lower lip, the curved upper lip, the inside of her bottom lip so much more sensitive than the upper.

Just touching her mouth made her insides tighten and turn over. Nerves and adrenaline and a hot, aching sensation low in her belly that made her want relief.

Relief, she repeated, even as it crossed her mind there would be no relief until she left Khalid and Egypt far behind.

It was the second night in a row that Khalid was woken by Olivia's scream. Tonight's cry pierced him and, racing to her room, he once again turned on the light, and once again found her fast asleep.

Troubled, he stood for a long moment in her doorway, the

moonlight spilling across her bed, illuminating her profile and the pale silk of her hair.

What was giving her the nightmares? Was it something from Ozr? Or had something else happened that she hadn't told him, something she wouldn't talk about in daylight?

He was still disturbed the next morning when he woke and dressed and joined Liv on the upper deck, where she was leaning on the rail, enjoying the morning sun. The soft breeze was playing with her pretty sea-foam dress, catching at the delicate pleats and making the hem swirl. The breeze was also playing havoc with her hair, blowing the silvery blond strands with carefree abandon.

She was as pretty as a picture, he thought, taking her in. Fresh, sweet and, after last night's kiss, extremely desirable, but he wasn't sure he liked this attraction. Didn't trust attraction, and definitely didn't trust emotion.

"Good morning," she said, turning her head to watch him approach.

"Good morning."

Liv gestured to a large boat passing. "I once booked a couple for their fiftieth anniversary on a Nile River cruise, but I had no idea there was so much traffic on the river. It's *busy*."

"It is busy, but apparently modern-day traffic is nothing compared to what it used to be. Until decent roads were built in the late nineteenth century, sailing the Nile was the main method of transportation. It's been estimated that in the Middle Ages there were thirty-six thousand ships plying the Nile."

"Thirty-six thousand?" she repeated, dumbfounded.

"The Nile is the heart of Egyptian civilization. Thousands of years ago Egyptians believed the earth looked like a pancake and in the center flowed the Nile River, while around the outside flowed the ocean. They also thought the sky was flat as well, and four poles held this flat sky up so that air and life could soar between earth and sky."

She glanced at a *felluca*, a small Egyptian sailboat, now passing their ship. "This is more beautiful than I imagined. It's so peaceful, and I love this area. It's very pastoral, very green."

"This entire part of the river valley is agricultural-based. You'll notice when we reach Kom Ombo—"

"Kom Ombo!" she interrupted excitedly, turning to face him, eyes growing round. "Isn't that where they have a monument to the crocodile god...oh...what is his name?" Reaching up, she tucked hair behind her ear, her white teeth biting her lower lip. "Sobek?"

He didn't want to like her, didn't want to respond to her, and yet her enthusiasm was appealing. She was appealing. "I'm always amazed at what you know about this part of the world," he said.

"Blame Jake," she answered, making a face. "He had a fascination with Egypt when he was a kid, probably from watching too many Indiana Jones movies, and acquired a huge collection of books on Egypt. In high school when his interests turned to girls, I laid claim to his Egypt collection."

"Smart girl."

She laughed, her blue eyes dancing with mischief and then slowly her smile faded. "Not that smart. I wanted to be an archaeologist but I didn't have the grades to get in to a top-notch public university, and didn't have the money to go to a really good private one. So instead of studying bones and digs I book travel packages to the Bahamas and Cancún."

"So go back to school, study what you want to study. You're still young. You've got time to pursue your dreams."

"You don't think I'm too old to go back to school?"

"For your information, you're still younger than I was when I started graduate school."

"What did you study?"

"Boring science stuff. Bones, dirt, digs, et cetera."

Her jaw dropped and her eyes widened, the sun painting her cheeks a soft rose. "Archaeology?"

"Mmm."

"You're Indiana Jones."

"Not quite," he answered, trying very hard to ignore her smile, her quick warm laugh, the way her eyes danced when she was happy. He'd never met a woman who made him hunger for more, who made him crave intimacy. He was the man who needed nothing but desert, sand and sun. He was the man who lived alone, a nomad dedicated to unearthing buried treasures, and understanding lost civilizations. He was a scientist, a scholar and a loner.

But Olivia was turning him inside out and he didn't want to be alone, he wanted her, to be with her.

She captivated his imagination, teased his mind, stirred his senses. Everything about her tempted him—her soft mouth, winged eyebrows, her golden silky tresses.

He shoved his hands in his pockets to keep from touching her. "Although I will say you're very entertaining."

"I used to make up stories to entertain Jake. He loved them, he'd laugh, but Mom didn't. She said one day my imagination would get me into trouble." She paused, her eyes suddenly darkening with shadows. "Isn't it funny how mothers are always right?"

Khalid frowned slightly, his eyebrows pulling. She was telling him something, he thought, telling him something important, too. He was a man who'd built a formidable career on bits and pieces. He knew how important one little fragment could be, knew every part was representative of the whole.

"Can I try to call home again later?" Liv asked abruptly, looking up at him. Some of the shadows were gone from her eyes. Some but not all. The shadows in her eyes added to his unease.

There were things she wasn't telling him, things that he needed to know.

What? he wondered, trying not to fear for her even as his loyalties were becoming increasingly divided. He'd always been loyal to his brother and family, but something in Liv called to him, something in her made him want to draw a line in the sand and protect her to the end.

"I didn't have a proper conversation with Jake," she added, "and I want to know how my mom is doing."

"Of course," he agreed, thinking it was a good idea because a call would occupy her while he did some research himself. "When we get back from sightseeing it'll be late afternoon here and morning there."

"Good. I'll call then."

He hadn't planned on kissing her again, not so soon, and certainly not in broad daylight, but with the sunshine playing across her face, warming her lips and turning her eyes to the same dazzling hue of the blue lotus, he couldn't resist her.

Clasping her face in his hands, he dipped his head, covered her lips, claiming them. Claiming her. As yesterday, she briefly stiffened, resisting, and then like yesterday, she gave in, melting into him.

Her surrender fired his hunger. Last night's kiss had been gentle and he wanted to be gentle now, but she tasted so sweet, and she tasted warm and she made him think of apricots and strawberries and he groaned against her mouth, deepening the kiss, plundering her mouth.

His body hardened and hardened again. Drawing her closer, he molded her body to his so that he could feel her slender curves, the pillow of her breasts, the narrow apex of her thighs.

He wanted her.

He wanted beneath her floaty, filmy skirts, between her pale slender thighs, inside her warm soft body.

Khalid felt fierce, carnal, *starving*. He hadn't wanted anyone, or anything, in years and now his desire consumed him. It was too raw, too explosive.

He needed her too much.

With a guttural groan he broke away, stepping swiftly back

to ensure he didn't reach for her again. "We'll go on shore soon. Make sure you have comfortable walking shoes," he said roughly, gazing off toward the shore, unable to even look at her.

Shaken, Liv pressed one hand to her mouth, feeling absolutely blindsided. What had just happened? Why was everything spinning so crazily?

The kiss just now was nothing like last night's kiss, either. This kiss had been hot, so hot, she felt singed, burned, her skin blisteringly sensitive, her legs too weak beneath her.

Last night's kiss had been so tender, so seductive she'd melted with desire. But this kiss punished. This kiss told her she wasn't in control. Not by a long shot.

Maybe that was what frightened her most. She had no control here. She didn't even know who she was here. Was she a prisoner, or a princess?

And standing there alone, she looked off toward the shore and spotted an amazing temple just there on the riverbank. "Kom Ombo," she whispered. They'd arrived.

The *dahabieh* anchored not far from the temple and Liv and Khalid walked the short distance from the port to the temple where they were met by their guide, an eminent Egyptologist Khalid knew and had asked to join them for the day.

"It is my great pleasure," the guide answered after introductions were completed. "Sheikh Fehr has helped me more than once. I am honored to show you one of my favorite temples because it is so unusual. Everything you will see at the Kom Ombo Temple has a twin. It is a perfectly symmetrical temple. Here, let me show you."

The guide couldn't have been more interesting as he pointed out how the Greco-Roman temple had been built with twin entrances, twin courts, twin colonnades and twin sanctuaries, but Liv kept glancing at Khalid, who was standing as far away from her as he could.

Why was he upset with her? she wondered. He'd kissed her.

Perhaps she wasn't supposed to kiss him back....

Perhaps he thought her too forward. After all, he was foreign. A sheikh. God knows what they wanted in women.

Frustrated, she forced her attention back to the guide and his description of the temple's twin sanctuaries. "The left, or western side, was dedicated to Horus, the falcon-headed sun god," he said, "and the right, or eastern side, to Sobek, the local crocodile god."

She glared at Khalid's back. Why wouldn't he even look at her? How childish was that?

Her temper suddenly got the best of her, so she marched over to Khalid and tugged on his linen shirt.

He turned his head to look down at her, his expression flinty, his rugged features set in uncompromising lines.

She lifted her chin, refusing to be intimidated by his fierceness. "You don't scare me," she hissed.

"Good," he growled, turning back to listen to his friend.

Liv stared at Khalid's broad shoulders and strong back before tugging on his shirt a second time. "You can't be mad at me."

He barely turned his head, giving her just a glimpse of his aquiline profile. "I'm not mad."

Not mad? He'd ignored her for the last hour. Hadn't spoken to her except for the introduction to his friend the eminent Egyptologist and acted like he was the only one of the tour, always walking a couple paces ahead of her, standing arms crossed as though he were some kind of impenetrable fortress.

She stepped closer to him. "I did nothing wrong. *You* kissed me. You can't be mad at me."

Khalid turned around so fast that Liv had to take a swift step backward. Khalid reached out, clasped her wrist and tugged her back toward him. "I'm not mad," he said in the quietest imaginable voice. "You did nothing wrong. We're supposed to be enjoying Kom Ombo."

"Then why won't you even look at me?" she asked, trying

to keep her hurt from showing. "You're acting like I've got the plague."

Khalid's dark gaze burned hot and he studied her for an endless moment before bending low to whisper in her ear. "I am trying to ensure you remain a virgin until we marry, *habiba*, but am finding it very difficult to keep my hands off you."

Liv colored, blood surging hotly to her cheeks. "Oh."

"Oh," he mocked, reaching up to caress her flushed cheek. "Now you see."

"Sorry."

"Of course you're sorry."

He stroked her cheek again, sending hot rivulets of feeling throughout her body. "Don't say you haven't been warned."

Blushing hotter, she dipped her head and moved away from Khalid, putting distance between them again.

He wanted her.

She swallowed hard as her insides did a crazy flip. Egypt was getting more dangerous by the day.

Their guide resumed his tour, leading them through the temple's damaged entrance, where he pointed out a small shrine to Hathor. The shrine, he explained, was now used to house a collection of mummified crocodiles. "Note the clay coffins," he added, pointing out the coffins. "They were dug up and moved here from a nearby sacred animal cemetery."

"Amazing," she whispered, overwhelmed. She was in Egypt, touring the very temples she'd read about fifteen years ago. She was sailing the Nile, exploring the old tombs, sleeping on a royal *dahabieh*. "Mummified crocodiles. Who would have thought?"

Khalid had heard her. He smiled faintly. "You'll like this next spot then," he said. "It's the small pool where the crocodiles were raised."

An hour later they were in a private car, leaving the riverside temple behind. Khalid had arranged for them to go to Daraw to see the famous camel market. Camels were being sold when they arrived, but it was a slow day, Khalid told her. Sundays were the busiest day with upward of two thousand camels exchanging hands.

"Who buys all the camels?" Liv asked, watching the haggling between buyer and seller with great interest.

"Most go on to Birqash, which is north of Cairo, and they're put on the market again. Buyers in Birqash will often send them to other Arab countries."

They stopped for a tangy frozen ice and found a toppled sandstone wall partially shaded by a towering palm tree where they could sit and eat.

"This is perfect. I was getting really hot," Liv confessed, savoring the cold, slightly creamy, slightly sour treat when she noticed that Khalid hadn't even tried his frozen ice yet. "You don't like yours?"

He looked at her sideways. "You have nightmares," he said gruffly. "Last night you had another one. You cried out, and it's not a small cry, but piercing. Disturbing—"

"I'm sorry."

He shook his head impatiently. "I want to know what's bothering you. What do you dream about?"

She searched his face, trying to see past his shuttered gaze. He had such a remarkable face, his low eyebrows straight above hooded eyes. His nose was long and yet it only emphasized the fullness of his mouth and that faint cleft in his chin. There were times, like now, when he was more rugged than handsome, but there were other times when he smiled and he became someone else.

She liked that someone else very much.

"I don't remember my dreams," she said, her heart suddenly aching. She wished she knew Khalid better, wished she understood him better. Maybe if he smiled more she'd feel easier around him. But she didn't feel easy. She was scared, scared of all the things she couldn't control. Like him. The engagement. Her future.

"How do you feel when you wake up?" he asked.

She thought for a moment. "Worried."

His brows lowered. The lines deepened around his mouth. "Worried about what?"

Looking into his face with his dark, serious eyes she felt a tug in her chest, another pull on her emotions. "Everything," she said, trying to smile but failing.

His frown deepened, a strong line appearing between his black eyebrows. "Tell me so I can help you."

Liv didn't understand the pressure in her chest or the tightness at her throat. She didn't understand the strong urge to reach up and smooth the frown line from between his eyebrows, either. It crossed her mind that Khalid frowned too much. He needed to smile more. "I'm okay," she said. "I am. Don't worry about me. You've worried enough. You've done more than enough. Now eat your ice before it all melts."

By the time they returned to the *dahabieh* it was late in the afternoon and Khalid gave Liv his wireless phone to use to call home.

But before she called, she took a shower in her en suite bath, rinsing off the day's dust and grime, and then slipped into a long, loose cotton shirt that reached midthigh. Curling up on her bed, she phoned Jake's cellular number and the call went through straight away. Unfortunately he was once again with their mom and unable to say much, but apparently their mother was doing much better and Jake was going back to work full-time now that he'd found a nurse to stay with their mom during the day.

"That's great," Liv answered, trying to be enthusiastic when in truth, she couldn't imagine her mom needing nursing care. How bad was the heart attack? And had the heart attack been followed by a stroke? But Jake wasn't telling and her mom didn't talk a lot, content to let Jake and Liv catch up.

After about ten minutes of chitchat Jake said he had to go to finish getting ready for work.

"I'll see you soon," Liv told them, blowing kisses into the phone and hanging up before she broke down in tears.

Things weren't right at home. Things weren't right here, either. She'd never felt so helpless in her life. What was she supposed to do? What could she do? The answers eluded her.

Exhausted, Liv stretched out on her bed, pulled the light cotton quilt up over her legs and fell asleep.

She was still napping when a knock on her door woke her up.

Sleepily Liv tumbled from bed to open her door. One of the ship's crew stood on the other side. "His Highness invites you to join him for dinner," he said with a small bow.

Liv assured the crew member that she would be right up, shut the door and glanced at her watch.

Eight o'clock.

She'd been sleeping for hours.

Liv dove into a celdon silk caftan, which was heavily embroidered and beaded at the collar. She wore narrow white trousers beneath the caftan and flat Egyptian-style sandals on her feet.

Worried about the time, she left her hair loose but did scoop up a pair of gold jeweled earrings out of the jewelry box to complement the exotic caftan.

She was upstairs in record time, taking the stairs two at a time, and when she reached the top she turned the corner so fast she ran straight into Khalid, colliding so hard she went reeling backward.

Khalid reached out and grabbed her, putting his hands on her shoulders to steady her. "What's wrong? What's happened?"

Bewildered, she looked up at him. "I'm late. I've made you wait."

Khalid's dark eyes fixed on her with intimidating intensity. "You're running like a madwoman because you were late to meet me for dinner?"

"Yes."

His gaze searched hers for a long, penetrating moment and then he tipped his head back and laughed, a huge deep laugh which made his white teeth and his eyes shine with a hint of tears. "*Habiba*, you make me feel like a king."

And realizing he was enjoying that she'd run at top speed to meet him, she shook her head.

"You're not fair," she said primly. "You don't play by the rules."

"The rules? And which ones would those be?"

"The ones that say desert sheikhs are barbarians that expect to be waited on hand and foot."

Khalid's lips twitched. "I think, little one, you need a new set of rules. Yours are outdated. Desert sheikhs today do not expect to be waited on hand and foot. They're far more interested in giving pleasure and making love." And, checking his smile, he gestured to the table covered in a rich violet silk cloth, and decorated with a low arrangement of dark purple lilies, completed by tall, thick cobalt-blue stemware. "Dinner?"

Dinner was entertaining. They were served endless courses of mouthwatering seafood and grilled lamb and seasoned vegetables followed by live entertainment. Musicians and dancers performed for them on deck and Liv sat on her pillow, an arm around her knee as she watched the swirling dervish of dancers. It was great fun to have authentic musicians and dancers on board and when they were finished Liv clapped until her hands stung.

"The trip just gets better and better," she said to Khalid after the musicians and dancers made their final bow and disappeared from the deck. "I'll never forget this trip, never in a thousand years."

He gave her a peculiar look. "We'll have more river cruises in our future."

Liv bit her lip. Did Khalid really think they were going to end up together? Did he really believe they'd ever marry?

Glancing down at her left hand, she studied the yellow diamond engagement ring. She was living the most amazing, fantastic and yet bizarre dream. She felt like Alice in Wonderland. She'd fallen down the rabbit hole and was having great adventures and lots of fantastic experiences, but she knew she'd soon wake and Khalid and Egypt and this beautiful river would be gone.

"What are you thinking?" he asked, tugging her toward him.

"Nothing."

"That's not true. You suddenly looked…sad."

"I don't know what's real anymore," she whispered. "I don't know what to believe."

Khalid dropped his head, kissing her lightly, fleetingly, and even as heat flared within her, his lips brushed her cheek, traveling with tantalizing slowness across to her ear.

Lightly he bit her lobe, his warm breath sending shivers through her. She squirmed at the pleasure, overwhelmed by her body's sensitivity. She had no idea her ear, or her neck, could feel this way and as his lips grazed the hollow below her ear, his tongue tasting her skin, she arched against him, arching so that her breast pressed into his hand, and his knee rubbed close to her thighs.

He rubbed her nipple, massaging it between his fingers until she felt absolutely wild. She wanted more, but she didn't know how to ask for it, didn't know if she could even ask for it.

Instead she turned her head blindly, trying to find his lips, craving his lips on hers.

His head lifted briefly, his gaze locking with hers and holding. His expression was so somber, so penetrating, that she shivered all over again.

As she shivered, Khalid dipped his head to cover her mouth with his. He kissed her as though he and only he knew the secrets of her heart, and he and only he could bring her out of the darkness. Reaching up, she clasped his face, savoring his warmth, the flutter of his breath, and the spice and musk of his skin.

She liked the feel of his mouth against hers, liked the way his arm pulled her close, liked the pressure of his knee between her legs and the crush of his chest against her tender breasts.

"We can't do this here," Khalid said against her mouth before lifting his head. "I don't know what I'm thinking."

"Then come to my room."

"No." He barked a rough laugh, his dark eyes lit with a possessive fire. "I'll walk you there, but only to lock you inside."

CHAPTER EIGHT

KHALID knew he'd lost his mind the moment he met Olivia, but now he was getting dangerously close to losing control.

Body burning, he followed Liv down the narrow stairs to her suite of rooms, his gaze riveted to the very feminine sway of her hips and the round, firm curve of her derriere. Watching her though was sweet torture, his groin growing harder by the second, his shaft already so erect it hurt to walk.

He wanted her more than he'd ever wanted a woman, and yet he wasn't going to take her. He'd never made a business out of deflowering virgins—especially since that seemed to be Zayad, his middle brother's, specialty—and with Liv's freedom at stake, Khalid was determined to do everything right.

At her bedroom door, he gave her a gentle push inside. "You'd better lock it fast," he said, his voice husky.

Instead she reached for him, catching his sleeve in her hand and tugging him toward her.

Liv knew she was playing with fire, knew she just might get more than she'd bargained for, but right now she welcomed the heat, especially if it would answer whatever it was burning her up on the inside.

"Five minutes," she whispered, feeling like the devil, feeling bad, wicked, but also knowing that once the truth came out, once everything became known, she'd never have this chance again. She'd never have him again.

"I won't make love to you," he said, even as she pulled him into her room.·

"Fine. Just kiss me some more," she answered, locking the door behind them.

"You're only going to drive us crazy."

"We're already on the way to crazy," she answered unsteadily, her legs shaking as she approached Khalid one nervous step at a time.

"You are going to marry me," he said, arms folded over his chest, his expression enigmatic. "It's not a choice. It's something we must do now."

"Can we forget marriage—"

"No."

She felt nearly feverish as she looked up at him from beneath her lashes. "Let's just forget wedding talk for five minutes."

"No."

"Come on."

"No."

She took the final step toward him, closing the distance between them, her thighs against his thighs, her breasts to his chest, her hands on his waist to hold her steady. "You want to kiss me," she whispered, her voice low and husky.

"I want to kiss you so badly that my body hurts," he answered, his jaw flexing.

"So do it."

He sat down on the bed and pulled her between his knees so that she stood before him. Watching her face, he slowly lifted her caftan and then kissed her flat stomach and leisurely took his time, kissing his way higher.

She gasped at the warmth of his mouth on her bare skin, and the tingling sensation of his mouth on her rib cage, and then at the sensitive spot just beneath her bra.

She gasped again when he kissed her through the delicate silk bra, and then closed his mouth on her taut, aching nipple. His mouth felt hot, wet, and as he sucked her lower belly clenched, and clenched again. She gritted her teeth, burying her hands in his hair as he sucked and caressed her nipple until she felt as though she were as wet and hot between her thighs.

His hands slid from her waist down to her hips, his thumbs stroking her hipbones through the thin fabric of her trousers.

She was making little whimpering noises now. She knew it but she couldn't stop. She craved his touch, craved release, craved satisfaction.

But then his mouth lifted and, holding her firmly by the hips, he pushed her back a little and then a little more until there was distance between them.

"Khalid," she protested, reaching for him.

"No," he answered roughly, as he stood and moved away. "You're beautiful," he added, his jaw set, his cheekbones flushed with deep color, "but I won't take anything that isn't mine."

Liv tossed and turned all night. Her body felt hot, wanton, desperate. She felt desperate. She'd never wanted anyone, or anything, the way she wanted Khalid, and yet she was never going to have him.

He wouldn't make love to her until they were married and she wasn't going to marry him. She wouldn't—couldn't—do that to either of them.

Waking early, Liv stripped her nightgown off and took a stinging shower, deliberately turning the water to a chilly temperature to try to cool her hot blood down. It sort of worked, too, she thought, shivering as she turned the shower off and grabbed a towel.

At least it worked until she thought of Khalid and his dark brooding gaze, and his full soulful mouth, and that hint of a cleft in his chin.

She loved looking at his face, loved that his nose was a little too long and his forehead a little too broad and his cheekbones a little too severe. She loved that he looked like a man and he kissed like a man. She loved that here in Egypt he'd woken something inside her, something she didn't quite understand yet, but felt powerful and fierce. All she knew was that it felt stronger than lust and deeper than desire.

Growing warmer by the second, Liv searched her wardrobe, looking for the coolest, calmest pastel shades she could find, eventually selecting tailored, sand-colored linen trousers, which she paired with a slate-blue jersey-organza petal top that came with matching shell necklace.

Dressed, she gave her image a once-over in the floor-length mirror attached to the back of her bathroom door and nodded approval. With her hair drawn into a low knot at the back of her neck, her bare shoulders now lightly sun-kissed, she looked composed, controlled, even disciplined, which was exactly what she needed to be today.

There could be no more kisses, caresses, stolen moments of lovemaking.

She was going to leave. She didn't know exactly when or how, didn't know where she'd go, but there had to be another way out of Ozr without further implicating Khalid. He didn't deserve to be dragged into her mess. He was a good man. He deserved better, and one day when he married, he deserved to marry a great woman.

Before leaving her cabin, Liv grabbed an ivory pashmina and then headed to the upper deck to watch the sunrise. One of the crew brought her a pot of coffee and some apricot-and-almond-filled pastries.

The sunrise stained the horizon the most tender shades of pink and lilac, making the ancient Nile Valley look young and new.

Liv took a quick breath, bewitched by the sunrise and the way it changed the sky, the water and the land. The Nile was magical.

But it wasn't just the history of the river that held her spellbound, it was the luxurious and yet authentic *dahabieh* itself.

The sailboat was in perfect harmony with the wind and sun, and there were moments where Liv was convinced she'd traveled on a time machine and had gone back one hundred, two hundred years, to a time when traveling was elegant, even sumptuous, with long lingering sunsets and cool pink sunrises and the wind blowing through the palms lining the river's great banks.

Khalid appeared at her side even as the captain steered the *dahabieh* toward the riverbank and dropped the anchor at Edfu, where they were to spend the day.

The port seemed exceptionally busy and noisy for a sleepy agricultural town and Liv wondered about the large crowd gathered on the riverbank.

"Are they waiting for a boat?" she asked Khalid as they prepared to disembark.

"No," he answered, studying the crowd, too. "My security tells me they've come to see you."

"Me?"

His eyebrows rose. "You're the new princess of Sarq, and they're curious to see my bride-to-be."

With the sun rising higher, the day was already considerably warmer and Liv took off her shawl and slowly folded it while studying the noisy crowd. "I'm not princess material."

"You don't know that."

"But I do," she said, dropping the scarf on one of the deck chairs. "I'm from a small town of thirteen thousand, and until you rescued me from Ozr, the most important man I'd ever met before was the mayor of my hometown, a man with some very mild celebrity status as he owns a car dealership and stars in his own television commercials."

He laughed softly, appreciatively. "But now you've eclipsed your mayor. You're a star, a celebrity in your own right."

Liv shot a skeptical look at the throng. "I'm going to disappoint them."

"How?"

She shrugged helplessly. "Look at me!"

He did, his gaze slowly sweeping over her from head to toe. "You're beautiful."

She just shook her head. She didn't feel beautiful. She felt like a failure, a walking disaster. "My mom raised us to have good manners, and of course she instilled in me good old-fashioned Southern hospitality, but royalty?"

Liv laughed weakly, thinking of the lessons she and Jake had been taught as kids. She and Jake were to be practical and pragmatic, honest and hardworking. They were supposed to do well in school, always be respectful, and never boastful. No lofty dreams in their family. No shooting for the stars. Just safe, steady jobs and safe, steady lives. "I know who I am, Khalid, and I'm a very simple person. I'd be ashamed of myself if I put on airs, acting like someone I'm not."

"Then don't try to act like a princess. Just be yourself, and you'll be perfect."

She looked up into his face, her eyes meeting and holding his. "Perfect for what?"

His gaze warmed. "Perfect for me."

The crowds didn't fully disperse after they disembarked, but they gave Khalid and Olivia space as they toured the Temple of Horus, the most completely preserved Egyptian temple.

Having already visited Isis's Temple, Liv was up-to-date on her Egyptian mythology and knew that Horus was the son Isis had conceived with Osiris, her dead, dismembered husband, and that Isis raised Horus in secret, so that he could later avenge his father's death.

Liv was most fascinated by the scenes painted on the Passage of Victory's narrow walls. The scenes depicted the fierce battles between Seth and Horus, and Khalid stood close by to explain to Liv the symbolism of some of the battle scenes.

"In this one, Seth has been turned into a hippo," Khalid explained.

"He's a tiny hippo, too," she answered, grinning at the artist's fanciful rendition.

"Seth's small size symbolizes his loss of power. Being reduced in size and shape, he has become less dangerous."

They walked farther down and Khalid pointed to the final scene, where Seth the tiny hippo was now a hippo-shaped cake and being eaten by the priests. "The priests eating the hippo cake is the ultimate statement. They've destroyed Seth completely."

She knew Seth was the evil uncle who'd killed his brother, Horus's father, but it was still a rather horrible depiction. "It's a sad end," she said, turning to face Khalid. "Hippo cake for priests?"

Khalid laughed quietly, and put his arm around Liv. "Let's head back. We can stop in the bazaar on the way and pick up some souvenirs if you'd like."

They hadn't done any shopping so far and Liv, not a big shopper, wasn't sure she wanted the hassle of the crowded shopping bazaar, but Khalid promised no one would push too close. "Everyone knows who we are, and they know I've security everywhere. They'll give us our space."

She'd seen how foreigners were treated in other touristy shopping bazaars, but was willing to give it a go if Khalid would deal with the aggressive sellers.

Shopping actually ended up being more fun that Liv expected. Khalid was confident, and comfortable haggling with the different shopkeepers. One vendor in particular caught her eye, his booth displaying absolutely gorgeous scarves. Liv stopped just to look, but Khalid, noting her interest, glanced at the shopkeeper, who quoted a price that made Khalid's eyes roll.

The shopkeeper tried again, cutting the price by twenty percent.

Khalid just stared at him.

The shopkeeper knocked another ten percent off.

Khalid took Liv's arm and they walked away.

A minute later the shopkeeper chased them down, four different scarves over his arm. "Please, please, Your Highness, I give one of these to you for your beautiful bride. My gift. Free. Please."

Khalid smiled faintly. "One is free. How much are the others?"

The vendor bowed his head, offered a price. "They're now half off the price he originally quoted me," Khalid said to Liv. "They should still be cheaper."

But Liv felt badly for the shopkeeper. He was trying so hard to make a sale. "But fifty percent off is good, and he's trying awfully hard."

"That's his job," Khalid answered.

"Yes, but he's offered a free gift."

"It's not free if we buy the others."

Liv glanced at the old man with his wrinkled little face and his bright dark eyes. "But we've helped him, right?" she whispered.

Khalid sighed and shook his head. "You are too soft," he chided, "but if you want—"

"Yes."

"Fine." Khalid spoke rapidly to the shopkeeper, who bobbed his head and hurried back to his stall to wrap up the scarves for them.

By the time they returned to the boat they were both starving and ready for lunch.

They were served beneath the canvas shade on the upper deck, and over grilled lamb and beef kebabs they laughed about their shopping experience.

"I have never bought any of that stuff before," Khalid said, with another wry shake of his head. "Most of it is junk."

"I know, but I couldn't resist the little brass statue of Horus."

"It'll look great next to your brass pyramid paperweight," he mocked.

She wrinkled her nose. "Okay, maybe I didn't need both, but how do you buy from one guy, and not the next?"

"Easily," Khalid answered. "You just say no."

They were still sitting at the table talking when one of the crew members approached and bowed. "You've a phone call, Your Highness. It is His Excellency, King Fehr."

Khalid glanced at Liv. "If you'll excuse me?" he said.

"Of course. I'm perfectly happy here," she answered with a smile.

And she was happy, she thought, leaning back against the cushions. She felt comfortable, relaxed, as though this boat—and this life—was really hers.

She was still waiting for Khalid to rejoin her, when she heard his voice and she turned around to welcome him back, but he wasn't on the upper deck. It took her a moment to realize he was actually one deck below, still speaking on the phone.

"We've just a few days left," she heard Khalid say. "The government has stepped up their pressure. I'm getting daily e-mails and phone calls now."

Liv frowned and leaned forward, trying to listen more closely. She knew she shouldn't eavesdrop, but she couldn't help herself.

Was Khalid really being pressured? He'd never told her. He'd never mentioned the calls or e-mails, either.

Chewing on her lip, she waited for whatever he'd say next.

"I know what I promised you, Sharif," Khalid was speaking again, "but she's not a criminal. I would never marry a criminal. You know how I feel about marriage—" He broke off, listened to something his brother was saying before continuing. "No, you're right. I never intended to marry. I never wanted a wife, but it's a little late for that. I've made a commitment and I intend to honor it."

Khalid's voice grew more distant. He must have been walking in a different direction and soon his voice faded away altogether.

Liv stared at the ruins they were passing, but the magic was gone. She couldn't see anything, think of anything, except for what she'd overheard.

Khalid and his brother, the King of Sarq, were fighting over her. King Sharif Fehr didn't want Khalid to marry her. Worse, Khalid didn't want to marry her, but would out of duty.

Biting into her lower lip, she tried to suppress the ache inside her chest.

She didn't want to marry someone who didn't want her. She couldn't imagine marrying a man who dreaded a life with her.

But what were their options? If Khalid was really being pressured, what could they do?

She could try to run away, but she wasn't sure how far she'd get, especially with no money, no ID and no passport.

She could try to convince Khalid to put her on a plane anyway, but then there was his honor and reputation.

The whole thing overwhelmed her. The problems kept piling up.

A few minutes later Khalid appeared at her side, taking a seat among the cushions on the shaded deck. For a long moment she just looked at him, trying to understand this man who'd risked everything for her.

For several minutes he said nothing and Liv clasped and unclasped her hands, suddenly nervous with him all over again.

Khalid fixed his brooding gaze on her. "Tell me what really happened that day you tried to cross the border."

Her shoulders slumped beneath the weight of her secret. There were times she thought he didn't believe her. Times she suspected he thought she was lying. "But I've told you at least a dozen times—"

"Tell me again. Maybe there's a piece you left out, maybe there's something more you can tell me. I have men working on your situation around the clock. My brother Sharif has had Sarq's top investigators looking for this Elsie, too, but so far we've come up with nothing. No clues. No direction. No progress."

Guilt weighed on her. "I'm sorry. I'm so sorry I got you involved in any of this. You thought you'd rush in, rescue me and be done with me. Instead, you're stuck."

His brow creased. "You make it sound like I'm some kind of victim, but I'm not. I'm not stuck or trapped. I'm a man. I chose to go to Jabal to help you, and I've chosen to continue helping you."

"But you don't want to get married."

He sighed, revealing a hint of frustration. "It wasn't on my personal agenda, but things happen. Such is life."

She studied him, seeing the creases at his eyes, and the lines bracketing his mouth. He looked tired, more tired than she'd realized, and her chest squeezed tight. "Why didn't you ever want to get married?"

He shot her a swift glance from beneath his lashes. "Who said I never wanted to marry?"

She'd tipped her hand, inadvertently revealing that she'd overheard him on the phone. Now she shrugged evasively. "You've made it clear that you live a solitary life in the desert, and I'd be lonely living so isolated in the desert, but you seem to like it."

"I've avoided emotional entanglements, yes—"

"Emotional entanglements? Is that how you view relationships?"

His shoulders shifted. "They are."

"You don't like people?" she persisted.

"I like the desert. It's peaceful."

"People aren't peaceful?"

Drawing back, Khalid stared at her hard. "You ask a lot of questions for someone who doesn't have a lot of answers. I think it's time we turned the focus back on you, and the hunt for the elusive Elsie."

Liv winced at his tone. She heard his frustration all over again. "She is elusive, isn't she?"

"Yes, and I don't understand it. No one has ever seen this person you've described. No border authority, no passport agency, no embassy official. And yet to get into Egypt you have to have a valid visa. You can't just enter without the proper paperwork but there is no one in Egypt—or any other Middle Eastern country—by that name or description. Are you sure Elsie intended to visit Egypt?"

"It's what she'd told me."

"But when you were all on the bus and you were stopped at the border, where did she go? Did she get off the bus? Did she get through to Jabal? What happened? How did she vanish?"

"I don't know. I was pulled aside and I never saw the others again."

He rubbed the back of his neck. "We need to find her," he said finally, bluntly. "The clock is ticking and your future—my future—depends on us locating her, getting her proper identity and verifying your story."

"And if we don't? Can't?" she asked, her voice soft, hiding her desperation because she didn't know how to fix this, or solve this, and she was scared now that no matter what happened, it was all going to end badly.

But Khalid wasn't answering her question and the fact that he didn't sent shivers up and down her spine.

"Do you think she has another name, or identity?" Liv asked quietly. "Is it possible to have two passports?"

"Possible, but not always legal. It depends on her citizenship."

"What can I do?" Liv looked up at Khalid, hating her sense of helplessness, and wanting to help, wanting to make things better but not knowing how.

He shook his head. "There's nothing at this point. But I'll let you know."

The rest of the afternoon was spent in separate pursuits with

Khalid attempting to work in his suite but ridiculously distracted by his conversation with Liv earlier and her impression that he didn't like people.

Was that the impression he gave? Or was she just attempting to draw conclusions?

Either way, her question and assumption troubled him. He wasn't an uncaring man. If anything, he cared too much, which was why he'd exiled himself to the Sarq Desert.

Losing his sisters had broken his heart. He'd loved them, adored them, enjoyed them more than anyone else in his family. More than nearly all his friends put together. Jamila and Aman were so smart and yet wickedly funny, full of laughter and imagination, love and mischief. The fact that they were beautiful didn't even come into it. It was their spirit he cherished, their love of life.

That subsequent loss of life was a wound he couldn't seem to heal. Not after one year, not after ten. He missed them and finally he accepted he'd always miss them.

But the love and loss had taught him a lesson he'd never forget. Loving others, caring for others, hurt. Thus if one was going to care, it was preferable to keep those that one loved at a distance.

While Khalid worked in his room, Liv curled up in the sitting room downstairs with a book. Fortunately it was a good book, and Liv read for an hour before thoughts of home intruded.

Lifting her head, Liv stared across the room, seeing but not seeing the ornate side chairs and leather ottoman. Her mother had warned against this trip. Her brother had warned her, too, but Liv had wanted something other than safe and predictable. She'd wanted change and had been thrilled by the prospect of going somewhere new and exotic, somewhere filled with tales of adventure.

She'd had exotic, and adventure, too, but now she couldn't go home—not easily—and it was devastating, especially with her mom so ill now.

If only she'd stayed home. If only she'd been happy with safe and predictable.

A lump filled her throat. Her heart felt unbearably heavy. She hated that her dreams now hurt others.

Hating her train of thought, Liv forced her attention back to her book and the rest of the afternoon passed relatively quickly, although Liv was glad when it was dinner hour and she could join Khalid on the upper deck.

Dinner tonight was unusually subdued. Khalid seemed completely preoccupied and once they'd finished eating, he excused himself, saying he needed to return to his desk. Liv forced a smile, trying not to let him know she was hurt or nervous.

She watched him start to walk away but suddenly couldn't let him leave. Jumping to her feet, she called his name. "Khalid!"

He turned around to face her. "Yes?"

Her heart raced. She gripped her hands together. She didn't know what to say. She just knew she didn't want him to leave. "I'm worried about my mom," she said, blurting the first thing that came to mind.

"Have you talked to her lately?"

"Not really. Every time I call Jake stays on the line and directs the conversation. I think he's afraid I'm going to upset her."

"Her health is fragile. Your brother is just trying to protect her."

"I know, and my mom only lost my dad a couple years ago, and now this heart attack. But I'm worried. I'm worried that something worse will happen if I don't come home soon, and I don't know if I can live with the guilt if anything did happen because of me. She didn't want me to come on this trip. She was adamant that I not go."

He looked at her a long moment before speaking. "So why did you make the trip?"

"I wanted to see the world." Her voice dropped. "I wanted to see what life was like."

Khalid stared off into the distance for several minutes before slowly turning his head to look at her. "Now you've seen it," he answered, his voice strangely hard, "and now you know the sacrifices we make to protect those we love."

CHAPTER NINE

KHALID disappeared down the stairs, and the staff immediately began to clear the table and cushions away, before dimming a half dozen of the antique lanterns. Once the deck was virtually empty, the staff gradually headed to the lower decks to tackle other tasks.

Standing alone on the semidark, deserted deck, Liv thought the night seemed endless. Mysterious.

The moon was only half-full and, closing her eyes, she took a deep breath, trying to calm herself, trying to relax. With her eyes closed, she focused on the sounds around her, listening to the water lap the side of the boat, hearing the breeze rustle palm fronds on the shore.

This is how it must have been to travel the Nile River in the old days, and right now she felt as though she'd stepped from the pages of a history book, or an E. M. Forster novel.

Drawing another breath, Liv opened her eyes and looked up. It was late and the stars glittered above, the sky so deep it looked glossy black, a sweep of onyx overhead. The warm breeze continued to blow, rustling the canvas awning, and whispered through another grouping of palms on the riverbank.

Tipping her head back, she savored the way the moonlight cascaded over the landscape, illuminating the swathe of river in brilliant white and silver light.

It was so bright that the fragments of towering temples lining the riverbank looked like they'd been hit with huge Hollywood spotlights, each of the sculptural shapes glowing in 3-D and taking on life of their own.

She could almost imagine Cleopatra climbing the crumbling stone steps and appearing between ancient limestone pillars and columns decorated with intricate shapes and designs, and Liv knew she'd never forget this trip.

Egypt might seem beautiful and magical with all its glorious history and Khalid might be a handsome desert prince, but what he wanted her to do, what he believed they should do, was as impossible as her becoming an Egyptian queen.

She wasn't from here, she couldn't stay here, she needed to go home. To her world, her family, her people.

She needed to go soon. She had to stop waiting for the right moment to present itself. Instead she needed to make the right moment happen. She needed to start looking for opportunities to make her escape. It wouldn't be easy, but staying here, marrying Khalid, would be worse.

He didn't want to marry her. He was marrying her out of duty. And she didn't want to marry anyone who didn't love her, who didn't passionately want her.

But then she pictured Khalid, and the way he looked at her, and that expression he would get in his eyes, and she felt a frisson of feeling.

No one had ever looked at her the way he looked at her. No one had ever treated her the way he treated her.

Maybe he didn't love her, but he did care for her in his own way.

Could that be enough for marriage?

Could caring and duty be sufficient glue?

Perplexed and ambivalent, Liv stayed on the upper deck to read, curled up in a chair, a soft blanket thrown over her legs. She read for hours even after the crew blew out some more of the lanterns at the far end of the deck, leaving just those near her lit.

Hearing footsteps behind her, Liv turned to look over her shoulder. Khalid, still wearing the white shirt he'd worn for dinner, walked toward her, but now his shirt was half unbuttoned, revealing the high, hard planes of his chest and the burnished gold of his skin.

He wasn't smiling and his dark gaze raked her from head to foot. "You shouldn't be up here by yourself. It's not safe."

His rebuke felt like a slap. "It's your boat," she challenged, hurt. "Your home. I thought I was safe with you."

"You are safe with me. But I wasn't here. And until we're married, you must be careful."

The wind was blowing and as she tipped her head back to see his face she had to catch her hair and hold it away from her eyes. "What if we don't marry?"

He stood taller, his shoulders thrown back. Making a rough inarticulate sound in the back of his throat, he turned his head sharply to fasten his burning gaze on her. "I won't do this now. I'm tired—"

"But, Khalid, we have to face the truth."

He threw his head back, lifting his face to the moon, and for an endless moment he didn't speak. Finally he said, "I gave them my word."

She swallowed hard. There was no compromise in his voice. No compromise anywhere in his stony features. "What if it's not right…what if we'd both be miserable—"

"I gave them my word. I have staked my honor and reputation on you."

Her insides hurt, her stomach cramping violently. Those weren't the words she wanted, needed, to hear. She didn't want to hear honor or duty, responsibility or reputation. She wanted more.

She wanted love.

Khalid took a seat next to her. "It will not be all bad with me," he said more gently. "I promise I will treat you with kindness and respect. I promise no one in my household, no one connected with me, no one who works for me shall ever treat you with anything but courtesy. You are mine. You are in my safekeeping, and I have made a solemn vow to protect you." His gaze met hers, held. "Forever."

She pressed a trembling hand to her middle. "And my family?"

"It is my hope they will come for the wedding."

"And after that?"

"You will live with me."

"In your...desert?"

"Yes."

"But would I ever get to leave? Ever be allowed to return home?" she asked, her voice faint.

His brow creased and his lips compressed. For a moment he stared off into the distance before turning his head to fix his piercing gaze on her. "Yes, you could. Eventually. After you give me my first child. But if you left me, meaning you chose to move back to America, the child would have to stay with me."

"What?"

He shrugged. "Our child would be heir to the Sarq throne. All Fehr children are raised in our country, in our culture. It is custom and law." Then he stood, and extended a hand to her. "Come, let me see you back to your room. It is late. I will not rest easy until you are safe in your room."

The soft swish of the wind in the palm fronds was the only sound as she followed him across the deck. As she slowly climbed down the stairs the wind whispered in the palms the same thing over and over. *You are doomed.*

You are doomed, doomed, dead.

Later that night Liv's terrified scream woke Khalid up, and this time when he went to her room, he turned on the light and woke her up as well. He'd had enough of the night terrors. He wanted to know what it was that upset her night after night. Wanted and needed to know what she was hiding from him because she was hiding something and he was beginning to fear the worst.

"What is it?" he demanded. "Tell me your dream."

Liv sat up in bed, her hair a mess, her eyes a bruised blue. "It's nothing," she said, but her lips were pinched and she was pale, too pale.

"I'm not accepting that answer," he said, walking around the bed and taking her wrist in his hands, where he checked her pulse. "Your heart's racing. You're terrified."

She just stared at him, her eyes far too big again for her face. It was the same look he'd seen when he'd appeared outside her cell in Ozr. A vacant, half-dead expression. The expression of one without hope.

"Olivia, I want to help you."

"I know."

"Then let me help you."

Tears filled her eyes. "You can't."

The despair in her eyes, the grief in her voice, hurt him. He couldn't bear for her to feel this way.

"Olivia," he said firmly, "I know you've been through a great deal in the past month, but the worst of it is over, I promise. We will find her. And when we find her, all this fear, all this worry will be behind us."

But that was the problem, she thought, searching his dark eyes. She didn't want Elsie caught, not if she was going to be dragged off to Ozr. Ozr was horrible, hideous and Liv couldn't send anyone there, much less another girl, and certainly not Elsie.

Maybe Elsie had committed a crime, but she also had a good side, and a big heart. From the very first day they'd met, Elsie had taken Liv under her wing, making sure Liv always had a safe spot in the hostel, a seat at the table. Elsie, fluent in four languages, translated everything for Liv.

"Let's talk about the wedding," Khalid said, changing the subject. "We haven't discussed our plans but we should, especially since we want your family here. I can send my jet over for them, and if a doctor clears your mom for travel—"

"She's not going to be cleared, not after a heart attack."

"Then it'll just have to be your brother. But at least you will have some family—"

"Stop. I can't do this. There's no point talking about weddings. I can't marry you. I can't, Khalid. It's just not right, and you can't make it right by forcing me into marriage."

"But I'm not forcing you. It's your choice, entirely your choice. The last thing I want or need is an unhappy bride. I've lived with an unhappy mother. I don't need a miserable wife."

She blinked, so surprised by the revelation that she didn't even know how to answer.

"And you're right, I might not be some Disneyland prince sweeping you to his castle on a white stallion," he added, "but I am offering you my protection. Perhaps it doesn't sound romantic, but safety, companionship and shelter are also important."

"I agree that safety and companionship are important, especially after what I've been through, but a marriage without love?" Liv drew a deep, shuddering breath. "A marriage that's based on a paper contract instead of emotions? How will that make anything better?"

"It'll save you from returning to Ozr, which could just possibly save your life."

She took another breath and this time held it, trying to slow her thoughts, as well as manage her emotions better because Liv knew when she was emotional she couldn't think properly and she needed to be able to think now.

"In theory," she said carefully, "we're exchanging one prison for another."

"I am not a barbarian—"

"I didn't say you were. But your culture treats women very

differently than my culture and it frightens me. I can't imagine living in Sarq and you've said that's where you live, and you've also said I'd live with you."

His jaw jutted with anger. "In my culture, mothers, wives and daughters are respected."

"Is that why you cover them with robes and veils?"

"Women are robed to protect them. We understand that a woman's honor and virtue is her most valuable possession so we guard it zealously."

"It's not just the robe and veil, it's the other loss of freedoms. I've noticed that in the Middle East women rarely go anywhere on their own. Instead they run errands and shop in groups, and many, if not most, of your marriages are still arranged, aren't they?"

"Yes, many, if not the majority, of our marriages are arranged, but we view it as a positive thing, and these arranged marriages are just as warm and real as the marriages in the West."

He sounded so reasonable, every bit the scholar and philosopher, but she didn't trust his argument. She couldn't accept that an arranged marriage brought the same joy—the same emotion and passion—of a love match. "Was your parents' marriage arranged?"

"Had to be. My father was a prince, soon to inherit his father's throne. His family spent five years looking for the right woman."

"And that was your mother?"

"No. It was another woman," Khalid answered wryly, "but she died unexpectedly just two months before the wedding and my mother was found as a replacement."

"No wonder she was unhappy," Liv muttered.

His lips compressed. He was trying not to smile. "My mother was thrilled—initially—to be married to my father and my father was very happy with her."

"So what changed?"

He looked down at her, his expression suddenly grim. "She never felt like my father's equal. He was royal, she was a commoner and it ate at her, little by little until she was obsessed with the fact that he had blue blood, royal blood, and she did not."

"Why would it matter so much to her? Did people treat her differently?"

"Some," he admitted.

"Your father?"

"No."

His swift, decisive answer made her brows pull together. "He respected her?"

"He loved her."

Liv felt a strange prickle of feeling. "How do you know?"

"He told me." Khalid's gaze locked with hers. "When he was dying he asked us, his sons, to always take care of our mother as he loved her and worried about her and dreaded leaving her."

For some reason his simple words nearly undid her. Emotion rushed through her and her throat ached, and her chest hurt, and she bit down hard to keep the intensity of her feelings from showing.

It was ironic, despite the distance between countries, and cultures, how similar people were, how similar love could be. When her dad knew he was dying, he had the same fear for their mom. He'd begged her and Jake to remember their mom, to take care of Mom, make sure she wasn't alone too much, make sure she went out with friends, and even dated again someday.

She blinked away the sting of tears. "That sounds like my father. He was worried about my mom, too." She paused. "But they married for love and despite what you say, it worked. They were happy, very happy, and that's what I want, too. I want to fall in love and feel like I'm the most important thing in the world to someone. I want to be special…cherished, and I want it to last. Not just for five months or five years, but forever, and relationships like that aren't from being forced together. They're from choice."

"So make the choice," he said quietly. "Stop fighting against fate—"

"It's not fate!"

"And get on with life."

"Right. Just marry you and move to Sarq and live wherever it is you live," Liv said hotly, sitting up in bed.

"That sounds good."

"No, it doesn't. I know nothing about you. My God, Khalid, I don't even know five things about you."

"Yes, you do. You know five. Try," he insisted, folding his arms across his chest and looking every bit the imperial warlord.

Furious with him, furious with herself, furious that she'd gotten them both in this ridiculous and yet tragic situation, she began to tick off what she knew. "Your name is Khalid Fehr and you are a member of the royal Fehr family."

"That's one and two," he said encouragingly.

She rolled her eyes. "You've an older brother and I think, but am not sure, that you live somewhere in Sarq."

"Very good."

She shot him a frustrated glance as she wrenched a hand through her messy hair. "That's not very good, Khalid, it's terrible. We've spent four days together now and you're still virtually a stranger."

"You know more than that, little one. For the past four and a half days we've had dinners and dates, and excursions."

"Dates," she said, rising up higher on her knees. "Did you just call our…sightseeing…dates?"

"Isn't that what you call it in the States? When a man courts a woman—"

"We're not courting."

"We should be since we're engaged."

Liv covered her eyes and collapsed onto her bottom on the bed. "You're courting me."

"Do you prefer wooing? It is an old-fashioned word, but perhaps it has the element of romance that you seem to crave?"

She peeked at him from between her fingers. "Can we not discuss this anymore? It's not going to help me sleep better."

He allowed himself a very small smile. "You fight this, you fight us, and yet it's natural between us. We are right together whether you're willing to admit it or not."

"How can I admit something I don't understand or trust? You are a mystery to me. Yes, I can see that you are a powerful man with a luxurious lifestyle, but that doesn't tell me who you are, or what you care about, or what you believe in."

Khalid didn't answer. He looked at her so long, his expression so intense and penetrating, that she felt as though he could see her terrifying secret.

"You know the real me. You just don't want to admit it because that would change everything, including your false sense of control." His lips twisted, his expression hardening, glints shining in his eyes. "Easier to ignore the obvious and play dumb."

Liv's jaw dropped. "That's not true."

His eyebrows rose. "Then tell me what you know, what you really know and I'll then tell you what you don't know. Fair?"

"You're an archaeologist," she said in a small voice, "and you come from what I think is a big family. Your eldest brother is the king in Sarq and he sounds as though he is a good leader and a good brother." She glanced up at him from beneath her lashes. "And you respect his opinion but you don't always agree."

She noticed Khalid's eyebrows rise. She'd surprised him with that one but he didn't contradict her. "I don't get the feeling that you spend a great deal of time on digs, anymore, but I could be wrong," she continued, trying to shuffle through all her memories and impressions. "You're compassionate and dislike injustice, and that's what I know," she concluded quietly.

He looked at her, eyes narrowing, jaw firm, and then he nodded. "Good enough." And then he left.

Morning came far too early for Liv and instead of bounding out of bed as she had on other mornings, she rolled over and groaned into her pillow.

She'd slept badly. Her head ached. And her stomach felt like it was a bundle of nerves.

And she hadn't even seen Khalid yet.

Burying her face deeper into her pillow she let out a muffled scream. She couldn't do this much longer. She couldn't. The stress was becoming too much.

By the time she dragged herself in and out of the shower and into a white eyelet sundress her mood had sunk even lower.

In the white girlish dress with her hair in a ponytail and red coral beads around her neck she looked sweet, pure, and it felt like one more nail in her coffin.

Glancing at her hand, she caught sight of her elegant yellow diamond engagement ring and yanked it off, unable to continue with the charade.

Tucking the ring into her jewelry box she left her room for the stairs. But as she climbed the stairs to the upper deck, her chest felt tight and her throat squeezed closed.

She couldn't continue here, like this. She had to go. First chance she got today, she'd leave.

Khalid was already at a table having breakfast and reading when she arrived on the upper deck. The table was a traditional table, too, one with four legs and regular chairs. There were glasses of juice on the table, a large pot of coffee, a basket of flaky pastries and more fruit. It was such a normal-looking breakfast table, such a normal-looking morning, that she felt the backs of her eyes burn.

This is what she wanted, she told herself. Normal. She just wanted to get back to normal.

Sitting down at the table, she glanced at the papers stacked in front of Khalid. Mountains of reading, she thought, glancing at the computer printout. "E-mails or research?" she asked, reaching for her juice glass.

"Both," he answered, looking up at her with a faint smile. "I have good news."

"You do?"

He leaned forward, elbows resting on the table. "They've found Elsie."

Liv felt like she'd been hit with a bucket of ice water. *"What?"*

"They're taking her into custody this morning and once they have her in custody, they'd like you to come identify her."

Liv just looked at him, her brain unable to process anything that he was saying.

"Amazing news," he added, with a shake of his head. "I was close to giving up hope."

He was talking and she was listening but she couldn't believe it. Couldn't. How was it possible? "Did they say where they found her?" she asked, her voice shaking.

"No," he answered, his head dropping to scan the e-mail in front of him.

"Or who she's traveling with?"

"No. Only that she's been located and they'll need your help to prosecute her properly."

She balled her hands in her lap, her heart thudding so hard it made her queasy. "Who told you?" she asked, her voice shaking.

He glanced up at her, a black eyebrow cocking. "You don't look well. Are you okay?"

"Yes." *No.* Biting into her lip, she felt anything but okay.

Khalid slid the top sheet of paper toward her so she could

read it herself. "It's from one of my detectives. He's been working in conjunction with the Egyptian police and since it's an Egyptian detective making the arrest, I imagine that Elsie's here in Egypt just as you said—" He broke off, his attention caught by her bare hand. "Where's your ring?"

She covered her left hand with her right. "In my jewelry box."

His forehead furrowed. "Why aren't you wearing it?"

She sidestepped his question. "I'll get it before we go ashore."

Her breakfast arrived and she focused on her fruit and yogurt, struggling to get a half-dozen bites down before she stopped eating altogether. "What do you think they'll do to her?" she asked, an unbearable weight on her chest.

Khalid looked over at her. "Send her to Ozr."

Oh, God. Not to Ozr. Not there.

Liv pressed her fingertips to her eyebrows, pushing at the terrible pain throbbing there. Her headache from this morning was just getting worse and worse while her stomach heaved.

There was no way she could do this…no way she could get through this….

Khalid pushed his paperwork aside. "Are you worrying about her?"

Eyes closing, she nodded, trying hard to hold back the sting of tears. She felt sick, so sick, so very, very sick.

"Liv, you can't blame yourself. You're not responsible for Elsie—"

"Ozr's a terrible place," she choked, cutting him short. "It's hell. *Hell.*"

"She didn't care about you," he reminded bluntly.

She could only shake her head. Things were bad, very bad, and they were just going to get worse. "I don't feel good," she whispered. "My head hurts."

"Do you get migraines?"

"I haven't had one before, but my head feels like it's going to explode now."

"Why don't you go downstairs, back to your cabin where it's cooler and darker?" Khalid suggested, standing. "Try to sleep. See if that helps."

"But aren't we supposed to go ashore?"

"We can skip Esna. Just spend the day on board, a proper cruise."

She lifted her head and looked at him, tears in her eyes. "Can we do that?"

"Of course." He frowned, concerned. "Liv, this is good news. Elsie's arrest changes everything."

She couldn't listen to any more, and she pushed to her feet. If she didn't get downstairs soon she'd begin crying here. "I'll be in my room."

"Good. Rest, catch up on your sleep. Tomorrow we'll explore Luxor."

Liv spent the rest of the morning in her room resting but when Khalid stopped by her cabin at noon to see if she felt like lunch, she agreed to join him on the upper deck under the awning for a light meal.

"You've been crying," Khalid said as Liv joined him on the deck.

Self-consciously she moved farther away from him, going to stand on the opposite side of the shaded deck. "I washed my face."

"I can tell by your eyes," he answered, dropping onto the low couch with the thick ivory and sand pillows. "How are you feeling?"

"Better," she fibbed, wishing she had a pair of sunglasses, something to hide her eyes from him.

"Come, sit here by me. We're having an informal meal. We'll just eat our lunch here on the couch."

"Aren't you hot?" she asked, leaning against the railing and lifting her ponytail to get her hair off her neck.

"You'll be cooler here on the couch with the fan."

But she didn't want to sit on the couch, and she didn't want to be close to Khalid. She was wound too tight. Wound to the breaking point.

"Olivia, what's wrong?" he asked quietly, not at all fooled by her attempt to avoid him.

"I think I'm just exhausted. I think it's good that we're just cruising today," she said, arms bundled across her chest. "I didn't realize how tired I was. Maybe we don't need to stop in Luxor tomorrow. Maybe we should just keep sailing."

"Not stop in Luxor?" He gave her an odd look. "But Luxor is the highlight of a Nile cruise."

"I know, but it's going to be hot and crowded, isn't it?"

"We'll have our own guide, our own private tour just as we have every other day." He rose from the low sofa and crossed the deck to stand before her. "I can't even believe you'd want to pass on Luxor."

"I've just had enough," she choked, her voice rising to a nearly hysterical pitch. "I've seen lots of ruins and monuments and it's enough—"

"Wait. Stop," he interrupted, cutting her short, before taking her chin and tipping her face up to his. "This is all about Elsie, isn't it? You're afraid to face her."

"Yes, I am afraid. I'm terrified."

"Don't be. I'm here, and I'll be with you every step of the way."

My God, he didn't get it. He didn't have a clue. "Khalid, I can't do it. I won't—"

"Won't?" he thundered. "What do you mean, won't? This isn't an option. You can't save Elsie and yourself."

"Well, I won't send her to Ozr. I can't send her to that place. I couldn't send anyone to that place."

"You might want to think on that decision, because it's you or her, Olivia. That's the choice."

CHAPTER TEN

SHE jerked her chin free and spun away from him. "I won't do it, I won't make the choice—"

"Then I will," he interrupted, his deep voice rough. "We are together in this, and I will not allow you to throw away your future, your freedom or your happiness."

"This isn't your decision to make," she answered hoarsely, bitter tears burning her eyes. "We're not together and we might be together now, but we're not a family. Your family is in Sarq. My family is in Pierceville. And those are the people we must be loyal to."

His dark eyes glittered. "I vouched for you."

"Then you made a mistake," she flashed, her emotions running so hot she knew she'd lost control. "And you made a mistake about me."

There, she thought. She'd said it. She'd told him. He'd made a mistake.

He took a step back, ran a slow hand through his hair. "We're running out of time, Liv." Khalid still sounded angry, but she heard something else in his voice now, a different emotion, one far colder, and darker and hollow. "The clock's ticking."

She'd begun to know his face so well and yet it looked different now. He seemed different. Remote. Detached.

"Let's forget Luxor," he said. "Let's just fly straight to Cairo in the morning and you can identify Elsie and then you and I can get on with our lives, and put this behind us before it spirals any more out of control than it already has."

"And if I don't identify her?" she asked faintly, perspiration beading her temple, her nape and brow.

"You mean if you *refuse* to identify her?"

She nodded stiffly, her heart thudding so hard it hurt.

"I'd return you to Jabal," he said without hesitation.

She couldn't look away from his eyes. "You would do that?"

"The Jabal government is threatening military action against Sarq. They want to escalate this into something deadly. I won't do that to my brother or my country."

Heartsick, she didn't answer, she couldn't.

"Something has to be done," he added wearily.

And still she just looked at him, too sad, too frightened for words.

But her lack of answer seemed to break something in him.

His features grew harder, colder, like granite sheathed in ice. "Knowing how I feel about my family and my country, how can you refuse to do this?" he demanded, his voice cutting and low. "Knowing that I have sacrificed so much for you, how can you not do this one thing for me? It would take five minutes of your time."

"Khalid," she choked, her hands clenching and unclenching. "It's not that I won't, but I can't—"

"Five minutes!" he repeated, his tone scathing. "Five minutes to identify her and we'd be done, gone from there. Five minutes and we'd be finished with this chaos and fear."

She was long past heartsick. She felt half-dead. He was looking at her with such disgust that her heart seemed to shrivel up.

"They hurt me in there," she said after an endless painful silence, "and they'll hurt her, too." But as she finished speaking, Liv could tell that Khalid wasn't even listening anymore. He'd turned his back on her to face the riverbank with the high narrow limestone walls. They were passing through a narrow gorge and the rocks rose high on either side, the rugged cliffs chiseled by thousands of years of sun and wind and rain.

"I thought I knew you," he said lowly, bitterness etching each word hard and sharp. "I thought I understood you—"

"She was my friend," she blurted, balling her hands at her sides in fists of sheer terror. "Even if she betrayed me, even if she did, I couldn't hurt her. Couldn't betray her. You must know me by now. You must realize I'm not that kind of person." Her eyes itched, burned. "I'm not vengeful. I'm not cruel. I wasn't raised that way and I can't change. I can't change who I am. Not even to save myself."

He didn't respond. He just stared at the wall of ivory and gold stone surrounding them even as her heart pounded wildly out of control.

Finally he slowly turned to face her. "You knew she had drugs, didn't you?"

"No, of course not—"

"So why would you protect her?"

"Because that's the kind of person I am."

"Foolish!"

"No more foolish than you," she railed furiously. "You come rescue me and you're a hero. But I try to help someone else and I'm a fool."

His upper lip curled derisively. "She had nearly a kilo of cocaine hidden in her cosmetics."

Her stomach rose in protest. "And how do we know for sure it's hers?"

"Because it was her bag. You know it was her bag. And surely you must have gotten suspicious when she never used the cosmetics—"

"But she did! When Elsie washed her face, or brushed her teeth, she used that little bag. She carried it everywhere...." Her voice drifted off as she understood what she'd said.

Khalid made a rough, mocking sound and Liv's eyes smarted. "Maybe if I'd traveled more," she added quietly, "maybe if I had more experience with different cultures I would have realized something was odd, but I found Elsie's eccentricities charming. I thought she was charming. I thought she was my friend. I liked her. I really did."

"And look what she did to you."

"Yes, look. It's bad. What she did was bad, but I can't condemn her, not to Ozr, not to a life sentence."

He looked at her without a hint of sympathy. "They're not going to just drop the charges, Olivia. Two governments have spent endless hours of manpower investigating this Elsie. My brother Sharif has been up night after night trying to find a peaceful solution, one that would free you while releasing Egypt from responsibility even as he ensured Sarq's safety." Khalid shot her a forbidding look. "Not an easy task."

She trembled inwardly. "Is there any way to get her freed?"

"For the love of God, woman!" he roared.

"I'm sorry, Khalid," she whispered, lifting her head. But when she looked up, she realized her apology had gone unheard. Khalid was gone.

Liv sank onto the low couch, shell-shocked. Although the canvas awning protected her from the harshest rays of the dying sun, she could still feel the shimmering heat and see the sun bronze the cliffs a darker gold.

She couldn't stop thinking about Elsie, couldn't forget the terrible darkness of Ozr, couldn't forget her own hopelessness before Khalid rescued her.

And maybe she was too naive, and maybe she was too trusting, but what if Elsie hadn't smuggled drugs? What if Elsie was set up? Blamed for something she didn't do? What if, and yes, this was a big what-if, but what if there never were drugs? What if the Jabal border officials made up the charges?

Liv's chest squeezed tight with grief and sorrow.

She couldn't accuse Elsie, or condemn her. She'd been taught to forgive, to forgive and forget.

But what about Khalid…and his brother? They'd all done so much to help her….

Drawing her knees up, Liv wrapped her arms around her legs and pressed her forehead to her knees.

Khalid had said something had to be done, and he was right. It was also her responsibility to do something. So what could she do? How could she fix this? How could she fix it with the least amount of damage? How could she minimize the impact for Sharif and the various government officials?

Accept responsibility.

Touching the tip of her tongue to her upper lip, she realized she needed to turn the lies into truth.

It would be hard, very hard, but at least she'd finally have a clear conscience. At least she'd feel like herself again. Good. Honest. Caring.

It'd be hard for her family, especially her mother, if she didn't return to the States, but Mom had Jake, and Jake would always take good care of her. Sons did love their mothers.

With a quick, deep breath she lifted her head, fixed her gaze on the rough rocks rising up on either side of the river and, drawing another breath, slower, deeper, she accepted responsibility. The sandstone cliffs blurred as her eyes filled with tears.

Maybe Ozr wouldn't be so bad the second time.

Rising, she went downstairs to sit at the writing table in the rarely used living room, opened the top drawer and drew out stationery and a pen. It took her several efforts to find the right words and the right tone but finally she was satisfied.

Sitting back in the chair she read:

To Whom It May Concern,
I, Olivia Morse, of Pierceville, Alabama, confess to carrying drugs illegally into Jabal from Morocco. I admit

sole responsibility. No one aided or abetted me and I am guilty of the crime for which I'm charged.

I write this of my own free will.

Olivia Anne Morse

Carefully Liv signed her name beneath the brief confession and, folding the sheet of stationery in thirds, slipped it into the envelope, sealed the envelope and then walked to Khalid's room where she slid the letter beneath his closed door.

The rest of the day crept by with agonizing slowness. For a long time Liv remained on deck hoping Khalid would return for lunch. He didn't. And then she remained, hoping eventually he'd come up for air. He didn't.

It was growing hotter on deck, too, and by three o'clock Liv couldn't handle the heat or her lack of activity and retreated to her room, where she lay on her bed and just stared at the empty space.

What was going to happen now?

What was Khalid going to do?

Frightened, she curled onto her side, her throat aching.

Lying still wasn't helping though. Her inner turmoil and tension just continued to grow, her cabin's four walls emphasizing the fact she was trapped.

There was nothing she could do right now. Nowhere to go at this moment in time. No one who could help.

Later that evening a dinner tray was brought to her room and after the crew member had gone Liv glanced at the tray sitting on the foot of the bed and felt an eerie flashback to Ozr. There her dinner was brought to her cell on trays, too, although dinner in Ozr was watery soup or lumpy rice and this meal smelled of mouthwatering seasonings and spices.

But still, she knew what a tray to her room meant.

Khalid didn't want to see her. He wanted nothing to do with her. Not that she blamed him. She didn't like herself very much, either.

She hadn't touched her tray when a half hour later a knock sounded on her door. Opening her door, she discovered Khalid standing on the threshold. The letter was in his hand.

"What the hell is this?" he demanded, shaking the letter in her face.

It wasn't the reaction Liv expected and she took an involuntary step backward. "I won't send Elsie to Ozr, and I don't want your country on the brink of war. You said something had to be done. I'm doing it." The words tumbled from her, one after the other. "This way everyone is okay. You, your brother, your country—"

"What about you?" he roared, dropping the letter and marching toward her to seize her by the shoulders. "What about you?" he repeated, shaking her fiercely.

He made her feel boneless, her teeth chattering together, but her pain was nothing compared to the anguish she heard in his voice.

"I'm doing my best," she choked. "I'm doing my best to fix this—"

"And break everyone's heart?" he interrupted, his dark eyes black.

"But I have to do this, I have to make things right."

His fingers tightened on her shoulders. "You've no idea of your value, do you? You have no concept of the depth of your family's love. Two weeks ago when I first contacted your brother and told him I'd located you in Jabal at Ozr, he offered to switch places with you. He told me he'd go there in your place. He insisted I negotiate with the Jabal government and allow him to be sentenced instead of you."

Khalid's eyes were no longer dry. He shook his head, his hold on her fierce. "He meant it, too. And I knew what he meant, and I suddenly knew who he was. Who *you* were. I knew what kind of family you were and I vowed to get you home to him, no matter the price, no matter the cost. It was the least I could do."

Liv's eyes felt hot and gritty and she had to blink to keep tears from welling up.

"I will honor my promise to your brother, because it is what I would want one to do for me."

"But why?" she asked, torn between fury and heartbreak. "Why do you care so much?"

"Because I know how Jake feels. I know how a man feels when he can't protect his family. I had two younger sisters and I loved them. I would have done anything for them, and I'd like to think that if they were ever in trouble, someone would have helped them. Someone would have reached out to them just as I have reached out to you."

"Where are your sisters now?"

"Dead." He said the word so harshly, it reverberated in the room.

"How? When?"

"Does it matter?"

"Yes. To me, yes, and obviously to you, too."

His eyes burned down into hers. "They died in Greece, on holiday. They went on vacation and they never came back."

"That's why you help people." She looked at him wonderingly. "You don't want them to suffer the way you've suffered."

"We have not come this far to lose you now," he answered instead before releasing her.

Khalid turned and stooped to retrieve her confession, which he promptly tore into a dozen strips. "The captain has the authority to marry us," he added tersely, "and has agreed to perform the ceremony tonight. The ceremony will be performed on the upper deck at ten o'clock."

Liv's mouth tasted dry as sand and she couldn't speak even if she wanted to.

Khalid walked to the door of her cabin but paused in the doorway. "I know marrying me isn't the answer to your romantic dreams but if it reunites you sooner with your family, then it is the right thing to do." He left the room then, shutting the door firmly behind him.

Alone in her cabin, Liv leaned against the bedroom door.

He'd had sisters, and they'd died and as though to atone for the sin of not being able to save them, he spent his life trying to save others.

It was mixed-up, messed up, wrong.

And it wrenched her heart in two.

The tears she'd been fighting to hold back, fell, and once the tears started, they didn't stop.

Sliding down the door, she sat on the ground and buried her face in her hands and cried as though her heart had cracked. And maybe in a way it had. Khalid, a prince, was giving up everything for her. What was she doing for him? Fighting his every move to try and save her?

She thought of Khalid as he had looked just before he walked out the door. So proud and fierce, so regal, so...beautiful. The past few months in Ozr had been a nightmare and then suddenly there he'd appeared, a desert prince determined to save her. He left her breathless every time he got too close. But he also made her feel safe. Protected. He'd believed in her when no one else here in this foreign land would.

Liv took a shuddering breath and slowly wiped away her tears.

She couldn't undo her mistakes. She couldn't change who Elsie was, or what she had or hadn't done. But she could make things easier for Khalid. If he thought the best course of action was to get married, she'd do it. She'd go along with his plans as long as it lasted.

Pulling herself together, Liv went to her en suite bath to bathe and wash her face and prepare for tonight.

The only white dress she had was the white eyelet sundress she'd worn earlier and Liv couldn't imagine putting that back on. Instead she looked through the extravagant wardrobe Khalid had purchased for her in Cairo. She did have several long gowns which would work. There was the pleated ivory-and-gold goddess dress she'd worn that first night in Cairo when the Jabal and Egyptian authorities came to their suite at the Mena House, but that dress didn't seem right, either, not with the memories she had of that evening.

No, she wanted to wear something new, something she'd never worn, things that couldn't be tainted with memories of anything else. Because this might be a marriage of convenience, but it was still a wedding, and even if it wasn't the wedding her mother had imagined putting on for her, it counted.

She was marrying Prince Khalid Fehr, Sheikh of the Great Sarq Desert, and she wanted to be beautiful for him.

Knowing she only had a half hour left until the ceremony's appointed time, Liv selected a creamy draped gown in the softest, lightest jersey fabric imaginable. The fabric stretched over her right shoulder, leaving her left bare. The fit was smooth, elegant, and molded to her breasts. A band of silky jersey wrapped her narrow waist and the gorgeous fabric, the color of French vanilla ice cream.

The dress wasn't white, and it wasn't stiff with petticoats and lace and all the things a Southern bride wore, but it was somehow better, more appropriate for Egypt and a wedding on the Nile.

Liv combed her hair into two braids and then twisted the plaits together low at the nape of her neck, securing them with little jeweled pins Khalid had given her. She'd thought the pins were exquisite, and yet also beyond ridiculous when she discovered the jewels were real—tiny diamonds and citrines studding the hairpins—but now, sliding them into her coiled hair, it was perfect.

She applied mascara with a very light hand, a touch of sooty gray eyeliner, a bit of rose-gold blush and a shimmer of rose-gold gloss on her lips.

Inspecting herself in the mirror she felt beautiful, calm, regal. She wore no veil. She had no jewelry other than her ring, which reminded her to get the engagement ring out from her drawer and put it back on her finger. She had no flowers to carry. All she had to give Khalid was herself.

With a glance at the clock in her room she saw it was time to go upstairs. Her stomach did a little flip, alive with nervous butterflies.

It's okay, she told herself, taking a breath and sucking her stomach in. It's just Khalid. Your desert prince.

Upstairs Liv discovered the deck had been lined with white candles. Pillars of white candles were everywhere, and the abundance of pure white light made up for the lack of any other ornamentation.

The wedding ceremony was short. The captain, a forty-year veteran of the Nile River, performed the brief ceremony. Their vows weren't just witnessed by one or two people, but all twelve crew members, who stood grouped behind them at a respectful distance.

The captain spoke the words in both English and Arabic and Liv answered when required.

Khalid wore a white *dishdashah* and a white *shumagg* with a black *ogal* to hold the head cover in place.

He looked fiercely beautiful, and extremely male, his broad shoulders dwarfing her, making her feel incredibly small and fragile.

She looked up into his face as he said his vows, lost in his dark eyes and the sensual fullness of his mouth. Then, vows completed, the captain declared them husband and wife, and legally wed.

With the ceremony over, Khalid accepted the congratulations of his captain and crew before escorting Liv from the upper deck, downstairs to his room.

Liv's calm disintegrated and suddenly she felt like a child dressed up as a bride. She'd never thought it through this far, but of course she should have. He was a man and she was a woman and obviously attracted to him. Obviously married, they'd take the next step…consummate the relationship, something he'd refused to do before, when she was a virgin and in his protection.

But everything had changed. She might still be a virgin, but in the course of fifteen minutes she had become legally his.

CHAPTER ELEVEN

PULSE racing, Liv followed Khalid down the narrow hall and when they reached his room at the far end, he opened the door and allowed her to enter first.

The lights were dimmed and the walls—painted a cream color and delicately stenciled in gold, apricot and teal, glowed in the flicker and shine of candlelight. Great brass candelabras covered the late nineteenth-century side table and there were more on the big mahogany bureau.

The suite felt like something from another world, the fabrics rich, sumptuous, and the furniture a unique combination of Egyptian and British antiques. Beaded pillows were stacked near the headboard, while a rich teal and crimson and gold spread covered the rest of the enormous bed.

Liv glanced at the big bed with the jewel-tone silk coverlet and quickly glanced away, growing warmer by the second, her gaze falling to the only place that seemed safe—the hardwood floor darkly stained and buffed to a glossy shine.

Khalid moved around the room, lifting off his head cover, opening the glass doors, turning on the ornate ceiling fan to create a stronger breeze.

Liv watched him, feeling very much like the amateur.

When he finally turned to face her, she was gripping her hands tightly, insecurity and apprehension getting the best of her. "I don't know how to do this," she confessed. "I'm sorry."

"Do what?" Khalid asked, moonlight spilling across him and onto the bedroom floor.

"This," she whispered, gesturing to his bed, the candles, his room. "I've never…you know."

Khalid saw the fear in her eyes and he felt a pang of remorse. He hadn't handled any of this well today, hadn't been the most diplomatic, either.

Leaving the door, he walked to her. Reaching her side he discovered she was shaking, and her fingers were folded together in front of her as if in prayer.

He nearly smiled, but again seeing fear in the hard set of her jaw, the firm press of her lips, the desire to smile faded. Tilting her chin up, he gazed down into those huge blue eyes, eyes the color of lapis.

"You don't have to know how to do anything," he said, his hand sliding along her jaw and down her throat, where he could feel the wild beat of her pulse. Her heart raced, drumming through his fingertips. He left his fingers there, covering that wild staccato. "I know what to do. That's my job."

In her long cream-colored gown, the soft fabric draped to highlight and reveal the elegant line of shoulder, the full curve of breast, the small waist and feminine hip. He was reminded of the glorious Egyptian god Isis.

Dipping his head, he kissed the side of her neck and the pale expanse of her jaw and then the corner of her lips. Her lower lip quivered and he kissed the quiver.

Liv shivered as Khalid's mouth brushed the corner of her lips. He was kissing her lightly, fleetingly, and she closed her eyes, and tried to relax by concentrating on what was happening now instead of what would happen *then*.

Then would be sex, but now was sensual, seductive, sweet.

With her eyes still closed, she felt his cheek graze her lips and she took a deep breath, drinking in the smell of him and that warm musk-and-spice-and-soap smell that was so uniquely his. He'd shaven before the ceremony and his cheeks and jaw were incredibly smooth.

As he caressed her, she lifted her hand to explore his throat and jaw, wanting to discover the very texture of his skin. Touching him like this awed her. He was so big, so powerful, and his face had the same strength in its very shape.

Lightly she traced the lines in his cheekbone and chin, along his jaw and across each eyebrow and finally the forehead. Touching him, she breathed him in again, her senses flooded by heat and spice and skin. It was like being in the bazaar again—the warmth, the seductive scent—and it was all the exotic beauty of him.

Khalid caressed the length of her, waking her entire body, making her ache and crave, her body tightening, her breasts peaking, nipples growing taut beneath the silky fabric of her gown.

"I love this dress on you," he whispered, stroking the flare of her hip, and from the small of her back to her bottom.

The hum of his voice in her ear was almost as much of a tease as the stroke of his hand over her skin. She felt hot and the elegant ceiling fan didn't seem to do much to cool her or the room down.

She gasped when Khalid lifted her long skirt to slide his hand along her bare thigh. His skin on hers felt even better than skin through clothes and she was impatient to feel more of his body against hers.

She moved her hands across the front of his robe, trying to figure out how to get it off. "Can we remove this?" she asked.

"Later," he said, his teeth lightly nipping at her neck. "First I want to know you."

He unzipped the zipper hidden in the seam of the gown; her dress suddenly came tumbling down and Khalid lifted her—naked except for silk panties, bustier and jeweled shoes—onto the bed.

Kissing her shoulder, he unhooked the lace-and-silk bustier and peeled it down, covering one suddenly exposed nipple with his mouth. Liv arched against the feel of his hot, damp mouth on her even hotter skin and reached up to dig her fingers into his hair, needing contact as his tongue flicked and licked her taut aching flesh. She wanted more, much more. He didn't seem to feel her urgency though, and took his time kissing and caressing both breasts, and then her rib cage and down her flat belly to the silk barrier of her panties.

As he kissed her hipbones he slid his hands beneath her bottom, lifting her slightly and making her insides feel so hot and wet she was afraid she'd melt in his hands. "Khalid," she choked as he stroked her mound through the now damp white silk.

He ignored the plea in her voice, concentrating instead on the incredibly tender skin on her inner thighs, his tongue exploring that small hollow between her inner thigh and the elastic of her silk underwear.

Liv didn't know if she wanted to push him away or trap him between her thighs when he put his mouth on her, kissing her through the silk, his lips covering, wrapping her tight, hard nub. She'd never felt anything like this in her life and she grabbed at his shoulders, her hands pressing against the thick muscle. When his tongue stroked down the silk to trace the lines of her inner lips she bucked, finding the sensation and friction overwhelming.

"No more," she begged. "No more, not like this. This isn't fair. I want it fair. You have to take your clothes off now, too."

He was slipping her silk panties off, and parting her knees, parting them to kiss her without the silk interference.

Liv cried out as his tongue touched between her, a light caress that became bolder, alternately licking and sucking until she felt drenched with her own desire.

"Please, please," she pleaded, her voice so hoarse she didn't even recognize it as she tugged on his robe. "Take this off, please."

The robe finally came off, as did the rest of his clothes. Heart in her throat, she watched him climb back onto the bed and straddle her. His body was a map of muscles and planes. She couldn't resist touching his abdomen, with the hollows and cuts in the muscle, and below his lean torso was a very big, very intimidating erection.

Nervously she touched the end of his shaft, the head surprisingly hot and silky in her palm. Curious, she wrapped her other hand around the thick shaft, sliding her hand from tip to pubic bone and then back again. His hissed breath caught her attention and, looking up at him, she saw the dark color in his cheekbones and the primal hunger in his eyes. He liked it, she thought, feeling surprisingly powerful. She could do something he liked and she wanted to do it again.

Gripping tighter, she stroked the length of his shaft, a little faster, a little harder, and she felt him tense, saw his thick black eyelashes drop, his lips parting in a silent groan of pleasure.

Abruptly he seized her hand, lifting it from his body. "You'd better stop," he growled, "or I won't be able to make love to you the way I want to."

Feeling very provocative, she linked her hands behind his neck and drew his face down to her. "How do you want to?"

He kissed her hard, deeply, passionately, kissing her until she shivered and danced beneath him. Lifting his head much later he answered, "Thoroughly."

And then he was kissing her again, stealing her breath and her body and her will. He moved her legs, his thighs inside hers, and as he stretched over her she felt the tip of his erection nudge her.

"I don't want to hurt you," he whispered, kissing the side of her neck, and then her throat and back to her lips.

"It won't always hurt, will it?" she asked, barely able to concentrate on what he was asking when his hands were on her breasts and his palms rubbed slowly across her sensitized nipples.

"No," he answered, dropping his head to suck one peaked nipple even as he positioned his shaft at the entrance to her body.

She tensed as his fingers brushed her damp curls and he soothed her by kissing her again. His kiss deepened as he entered her slowly. Fortunately her body was wet and welcoming and only once did the pressure become too much. She pressed at his chest, holding her breath, feeling panicky.

"Hurts?" he murmured in her ear.

She nodded, afraid to exhale.

"Look at me," he said, smoothing her hair back from her brow.

She did, and what she saw in his face—in his eyes—made her clasp his face and kiss him, kiss him to tell him how much it mattered, how much she appreciated everything he was and everything he'd done.

And, kissing him, her heart exploded wide open and her body accepted him and he was with her, completely with her making her feel more than she'd ever felt in her life.

Khalid, she whispered as his powerful body surged into hers, *my husband*.

The first time they made love she didn't have an orgasm. The second time they made love she had two, and after shattering against his hard, sinewy body a second time, Liv felt as though she, and her life, had been turned inside out and upside down.

Khalid had changed her. Khalid hadn't taken her virginity, he'd made her feel cherished and beautiful. He'd made her feel like a woman.

In the morning breakfast was brought to her in bed and Liv dragged herself into a sitting position only to discover she was ridiculously sore. Khalid, hearing her whimper, appeared from the en suite bath where he'd just finished showering and dressing.

"What's wrong, little one?" he asked, buttoning his linen shirt.

She grimaced as she adjusted the tray on her lap. "I'm a trifle sore, thanks to your not-so-little one."

He grinned, obviously pleased, and Liv shook her head, amazed at the male ego. "So what are our plans?" she asked. "I wasn't sure what was going to happen today. Do we have to go somewhere, do something to formalize the wedding?"

"No, we'll finish the cruise as planned, here in Luxor," he answered. "I love Luxor. It's my favorite Egyptian city, and my Egyptian friends know it's my favorite city and they expect us here today. But dress in something cool," he said, leaning over the bed to kiss her. "The Valley of the Kings can get hot."

Liv had read that Luxor was the world's greatest open-air museum and she immediately understood the significance when presented with the Theban necropolis to view the royal tombs.

Luxor, with its wealth of monuments, ranging from the Valleys of the Kings and Queens to the Colossi of Memncon, was old Egypt, deep Egypt like the one she'd read about in Jake's books.

Their guide was another good friend of Khalid's and he'd gotten them access to the Tomb of Nefertari, which strictly limited the number of visitors to protect the fragility of the ancient tomb.

It was a hot day already, even hotter inside the tomb, and Liv began to wilt. Their guide was exceptional, but very detail-oriented and as the temperature in the tomb continued to climb her discomfort increased.

Once Khalid looked at her, a questioning light in his eyes, but she forced a quick smile, not wanting to worry him, especially when she knew how much he enjoyed this particular tomb.

But his gaze held hers longer than necessary and she felt her chest squeeze tight, her heart filled with the most bittersweet emotion imaginable.

If only she'd met Khalid in different circumstances.

If only they'd met on an airplane or on a street corner in passing. If only, she thought wistfully…

From the Valley of the Queens they traveled on to the Valley of the Kings and it was even hotter by the time they faced the first set of stairs, due to the sun rising high in the sky.

"Why were the royal tombs built here?" Liv asked the guide, fanning herself, as they paused part way on the flight of steps. The Valley of the Kings was all desert, barren limestone rock and sizzling heat.

"Some believe the tombs were carved out of the mountains to help with the journey to the afterworld," the guide answered, "and others think that once the first tomb was built here, it just became the popular thing to do."

"Either way," Khalid suddenly added, arms crossed, "the Egyptians' mummy specialists definitely knew the desert was an ideal place to store a corpse."

She shuddered. "Yuck."

"But that's what these are, little one. There are sixty-two tombs opened. They expect there are still that many to discover."

"That's a lot of dead bodies."

He laughed softly and they continued hiking, climbing eighty steps up one of the mountains before creeping down through a huge cave that smelled musty and dank.

Liv wrinkled her nose as they squeezed through uncomfortably narrow passages. She didn't like the close confines, particularly coupled with the mind-boggling temperatures. Liv told herself that it would soon pass, but as the guide led them deeper into the tomb Liv felt like she was suffocating. She couldn't catch her breath and her head was beginning to spin again.

"Too hot?" Khalid's voice murmured close to her ear and she nodded, feeling yet another spike in temperature, aware all over again of Khalid's large, hard frame so close to her own.

"A little," she admitted.

"Let's go out," he said, touching her low on her back. "We've seen enough."

His light touch flooded her veins with fire, her body remembering him, her body already craving him. "No. No, this is incredible. I've never seen anything like it and if I leave now, I might never have the chance to see it again."

"All right," he agreed reluctantly, and they reached the bottom of the cave without further incident.

On reaching the bottom, Liv understood why this tomb was such a favorite of tourists. Oval-shaped, the tomb was exquisitely painted with astonishing hieroglyphics on every wall, while the ceiling was a gorgeous azure blue.

Liv stared up in awe. "It's beautiful."

"It is," Khalid agreed.

Liv lingered behind Khalid and the guide to have a closer look at the hieroglyphics. Other tourists were in the tomb, too, and there was some gentle jostling as everyone jockeyed to see the decorations that illustrated the ancient Egyptians' thoughts and ideas and expectations for the afterworld.

Bumped twice by a particularly aggressive tourist, Liv was just about to return to Khalid's side when a uniformed Egyptian took her arm. "Ma'am, please step away from your group and come with me."

"I'm sorry," Liv said, trying to tug her arm free. "I don't understand. What's wrong?"

"Just come with me, ma'am."

Absolutely stunned, Liv's stomach fell even as she experienced the most painful déjà vu. She'd been through this before, she'd been hauled off the bus in Jabal and it'd gone from confusing to terrifying in less than twelve hours. Now she feared the worst. Why had she been singled out? What was happening?

Khalid suddenly appeared at her side. "Take your hand off her now."

The uniformed officer bowed. "Your Highness, forgive me, it's for your protection."

Khalid's eyes narrowed. "You dare to suggest that I need to be protected from my own woman?"

"Your Highness, we have observed suspicious activity in the

tomb today and believe Miss Morse is involved in illegal activity here."

Khalid's features hardened, his dark eyes glittered. "Do you have proof?"

"If we could check her bag."

"If you were in my country, I'd have you hanged for your insolence."

The official sweated even more profusely. "We respectfully request permission to go through her belongings."

"No."

"Your Highness."

"You've insulted my wife, you've insulted my family and you've insulted me. I suggest you call your chief of police because there is going to be hell to pay."

The guards stepped back to confer and Khalid reached out to take Olivia's hand in his. "No one will touch you," he murmured. "No one will take you from me. I promise."

She clung to his hand. "Khalid, you must believe me. I wouldn't take anything. I'm not a thief. I'm not a drug smuggler."

"I know."

"Do you?" Her gaze searched his. "Do you really? Because there's no way I could do what they say—" She broke off as the officers returned.

"Your Highness, if you and Miss Morse—"

"*Princess* Fehr," Khalid corrected.

"If you and Princess Fehr would follow us, a helicopter is coming to take us to the police station."

The helicopter transported them from the sweltering Valley of the Kings to Luxor's police station, where the chief of police awaited along with a half dozen other officials. Khalid greeted three of them by name and as it turned out, two of the officials were from Sarq, the third an Egyptian lawyer who was close friends with the Fehr family.

Liv was seated in a small room just around the corner from the conference room. She couldn't see everyone, but she could hear the voices and she knew from Khalid's tone that he was very, very angry.

The meeting in the conference room lasted less than an hour and when it was finished, Khalid took her hand and walked out of the police station without looking back.

They climbed into another helicopter, this one sent by King Sharif Fehr for their use. "What happened in there?" she asked, catching sight of Khalid's grim expression. "What's going to happen now?"

"Nothing."

She leaned forward. "What do you mean, nothing?"

"It's over."

"What about Elsie? What's happening to her?"

"They've dropped the charges and she's being sent home tonight."

She looked at him, her brow deeply furrowed. "So there were no drugs? She was falsely accused?"

"I don't know, and I don't know if we'll ever know. But the fact that someone from Jabal would attempt to plant drugs on you here raised so many red flags that the entire case has been dismissed."

She said nothing for a moment. "The case wouldn't have been dismissed, though, if it weren't for you. You didn't just save me once, you saved me twice."

He shrugged uncomfortably. "I promised to protect you."

"You helped Elsie, too."

He shot her a sideways glance. "You wanted me to, didn't you?"

"Yes."

They flew to Cairo, where they boarded the Fehr royal jet. As the jet taxiied down the runway and then lifted off, Liv was briefly blinded by the setting sun's brilliance, the long, late afternoon rays turning the desert orange and red as though the sand itself was on fire.

Egypt had been riveting from start to finish, she thought, biting into her lower lip as the plane's wings tipped, blocking the view below.

They were served a meal, and Liv could only pick at her salad. Khalid was silent and he didn't eat, either. The flight attendant didn't comment as she cleared their virtually untouched plates.

"Are we going to Sarq?" Liv asked Khalid after their table had been removed.

He'd been staring out the window since takeoff, his gaze shuttered, his expression strangely remote. "Not yet." He hesitated. "I have some things to take care of first."

Liv watched him covertly, worried. He hadn't been the same since the accusation in the tomb and she wished she knew what he was thinking. Was he mad at her? Embarrassed? Disappointed?

"Are you mad at me?" she asked uncertainly.

"No."

"But at the Valley of the Kings—"

"It's over."

His short, terse answers did little to relieve her anxiety. Something was bothering him. But what?

She longed to press for a real answer, but at the same time didn't feel entitled to push him. He'd done so much for her, helped so much she felt she needed to respect his need for space…privacy. If he wanted to talk to her, he could. He would. He'd never had a problem talking to her in the past.

And yet as the flight passed with no interaction between them her sense of isolation grew.

For the first time she realized she could handle him being mad at her. She could even handle him not talking to her. But she couldn't handle not knowing what he was thinking.

She didn't like being shut out. It hurt.

It was dark by the time they arrived in Paris and raining. It wasn't a freezing rain, but Liv still felt chilled as they crossed the airport tarmac to enter the stylish executive terminal.

As always a chauffeured car waited, this time a beautiful dark gray Bentley that swiftly transported them to the historic and sumptuous Hotel Ritz.

They dined in their room, the presidential suite, served by their own personal waiter. Khalid was even more remote during dinner and Liv felt increasingly alarmed.

In the past eight hours he'd built a wall around himself and from what she saw, he wasn't going to let her over, or through. At least not yet.

At bedtime Liv didn't know what to do. They'd only been married one day and one night, and last night had been her first night sharing a man's bed. She didn't know what to expect tonight and, after changing into her white nightdress edged with pink lace, she stood uncertainly in the middle of the bedroom.

Khalid appeared in the doorway, his brow furrowing as he looked at her.

"You are angry with me," she said huskily, her fingers twisting together, a nervous habit she'd never been able to break. "Tell me what I did so I won't do it again."

"It's not you."

"Khalid—"

"I think it's better if we don't talk tonight," he interrupted emotionlessly. "I'll sleep on the couch in the living room. It folds out into a bed. The butler has already put sheets on it for me."

Liv fought to hang on to her composure. "But why are you sleeping there? Why aren't you sleeping with me?"

"A lot has happened this week."

"Yes."

"I think we could both use some alone time."

"I don't."

He shrugged. "I disagree. You've been through a lot, little

one. Your head is spinning so fast you don't even know if you're coming or going."

She stared at the rose-and-gold patterned carpet with the bits of royal blue. "You're sorry you married me."

"It shouldn't have been under those conditions, no."

"But it was under those conditions," she answered, lifting her head, meeting his gaze.

"Something I regret."

"Why?"

"No woman should be forced into marriage. Last night I forced you—"

"You didn't!"

"I'm deeply sorry. I wanted to protect you—"

"And you did." She crossed to him, reached out with both hands to his arm. He was warm and solid and yet he felt even more distant than before. He was disappearing before her eyes, becoming a stranger all over again. "Khalid, all you've done is help me."

"Good." And, bending his head, he kissed her on the cheek near her mouth, the feel of his lips sending electric sparks throughout her body. "Sleep well. And no more bad dreams tonight."

She watched him turn and leave. "I don't have them anymore," she said, calling after him.

He hesitated in the doorway. "Why not?"

"You made them go away."

CHAPTER TWELVE

AFTER a fitful night's sleep, Liv didn't want to get out of bed but Khalid pushed open the curtains, waking her. "Feel like seeing Paris?" he asked.

She pushed up onto her elbow, looked out the window and saw the rain. "It's raining."

"It always rains in Paris. Come, get up, get dressed. We'll go have breakfast and explore the city. You'll enjoy it. You can't come to Paris without seeing something."

He seemed so much like his old self that Liv couldn't help smiling back. He'd apparently resolved whatever was bothering him yesterday. "Give me a half hour to shower and dress."

"I'll order you some coffee."

He disappeared and Liv jumped from bed, excited to discover Paris with Khalid. He'd made Egypt magical. Imagine what he could do for the most romantic city in the world.

The morning passed quickly. After a breakfast in a charming café, they were then off to see some of Khalid's favorite historic sites including the nearby Place de la Concorde—site of the infamous guillotine—and then down the Champs-Élysées, the seventeenth-century garden promenade that had become an avenue connecting the Concorde and the Arc de Triomphe.

The rain let up as they wandered around Montparnasse, with

its artist studios, music halls and café life, but by the time they reached the Eiffel Tower, it'd started again, the skies a steely gray.

"I'm too wet," Liv protested with a laugh, getting drenched despite the umbrella Khalid had carried over their heads.

He stopped on the pavement and pushed a wet tendril of hair from her cheek. "Yes, you are." He looked at her so long, his expression intense. "Time to go."

Stepping into the street, he hailed a taxi cab, one of the many that flooded the streets of Paris. The taxi pulled alongside the curb and Khalid opened the back door.

"Go," he said, gesturing for her to get in.

She just stood there, beneath his umbrella in the pouring rain. "Go?" she asked dumbly, hearing the *ping ping* of the rain on the umbrella. "What do you mean, go? Go where? Go do what?"

"Go home. Go back to where you belong."

She reached up to wipe a wet splash from her cheek. "But we're married—"

"It can be annulled. You were coerced into marrying me. It wouldn't stand up in court."

But what about me? she wanted to ask. What about us? Instead she grasped for straws. "What about Jabal? Won't their government go after you? Won't they try to ruin you—"

"It's been dismissed. It's all over. But even if it wasn't, they can't ruin me." His lips curved, twisting. "I'm too powerful for them to ruin."

"But your name…and that whole issue of honor. If I leave you, won't that hurt you and your reputation?"

He shrugged. "You left me. You ran away. What am I to do?"

The taxi driver stuck his head out the window. "Come on, come on, I don't have all day."

Khalid's dark eyebrows lifted and, looking down at Olivia, he smiled that wry, heart-wrenching smile of his. "He's in a hurry, little one. You'd better go."

Olivia couldn't believe this was happening. It's what she'd

wanted, it's what she'd fought so hard for, and yet now that she had it, now that it was happening, she didn't understand it. Wasn't ready for it at all, wasn't even sure it was right. Khalid had never been her jailer. He was her rescuer, her hero.

She gave her head a slight shake. "I don't know—"

"Go to the U.S. embassy. They're expecting you. They know the story. You've just managed to escape from me and you've nothing on you—no wallet, no passport, just the clothes on your back—and you must get home. They'll see you home."

"But surely my ticket—"

"Paid for."

"My passport."

"Taken care of."

Her eyes burned. He'd been planning this for a while then. He'd known all along he was going to release her. And yet he'd never let on. He'd played his part, played it all the way out.

"Why?" she whispered, wanting to touch him, wanting to wrap her arms around him and feel his warmth and strength and courage.

His courage. Perhaps the thing she loved best about him.

He shrugged. "It's what I'd want someone to do for my sisters." And then he gave her a gentle push into the cab. "Be careful out there, princess. Remember that there are many wolves in sheep's clothing."

Before she even knew how, she was seated in the backseat, the umbrella folded and put away. Rain slashed down in long wet streaks. Liv leaned out the open door, pushing a wet sticky strand of hair from her face. "Will I ever see you again?"

Khalid's dark gaze met hers and held. "Maybe."

"Only maybe?"

"If you need me." And then he bent, cupped her cheek and kissed her lips, slowly, tenderly, before stepping back and slamming the taxi door closed.

The taxi sped off and Olivia turned and stared out the back

window through the slashing rain. She caught Khalid's profile before he turned away and then another car was behind them and he disappeared from sight altogether.

The flight from Paris to New York was endless. Khalid had bought her a first-class ticket on Air France, which meant her seat became a real bed with real sheets and blankets and not just one, but two very soft down pillows.

She practically had a flight attendant to herself. The flight attendant served her a five-course dinner and glasses of wine and champagne, but even with all the amenities and attentive service Liv couldn't stop thinking.

Or feeling.

She'd only just gotten married—a bride of only two days— and now it was already over.

Pulling the blanket to her nose, she pressed the soft fleece to her mouth and tried to think of something else. Tried to think of anything but the man she'd married and the man who'd sent her home.

But it's what you wanted, she reminded herself. *You made it clear that your family was in Pierceville and that's where you belonged.*

Had she been wrong?

In New York Liv caught yet another flight, this one bound for Arkansas, where her brother would meet her plane and drive her the three hours home.

During the flight to Arkansas she once again tried not to think, tried not to remember, not the fiery sands of Egypt or the towering pyramids or the mirage-like Nile winding through the fertile river valley.

She wouldn't remember the man who appeared outside her cell like an avenging angel sent from heaven to bring her home.

She wouldn't remember how he faced down an entire country to secure her release.

She wouldn't remember his dark eyes and the expression in them when he looked at her.

And most of all she wouldn't remember how it felt to be in his arms when he held her close. She wouldn't remember the thick, smooth muscles of his chest or the hard thighs or the flat abdomen or the warmth of his golden skin as he covered her, moved over her, filling her.

She wouldn't remember that she'd come so close to losing her heart completely, wouldn't remember that she'd been just one kiss away from being lost to his desert and his power forever.

Her plane touched down in Arkansas without a bump, the landing so smooth that it wasn't until they were drawing up to the gate that she'd registered that they'd landed. She was home.

With all the security headaches in American airports, she knew Jake would have to wait until she exited to baggage claim, It was as she was walking toward the baggage carousel that she heard him say, "If you aren't a sight for sore eyes."

Jake, she thought. She turned around and looked up into the bluest eyes in the world. Tall, handsome and kind, he was the best brother, and she threw herself in his arms, hugging him hard, hugging him to make up for all the things she could never tell him. He'd never understand what had happened to her these past six weeks, and she didn't want him to understand. It'd just upset him more and they'd all been through enough.

It was time to move on. Time to get their lives back to normal.

"Mom's dying to see you," he said gruffly when he finally let her go. "She wanted to come but I didn't think she needed a six-hour drive."

"But she's doing better?" she asked as Jake took her carry-on bag off her shoulder and slipped it over his.

"Much better."

"Good."

He looked her up and down, taking in her slim navy sleeveless dress, which she was wearing with knee-high black suede boots with a small kitten heel. "You're all grown-up," he said, stepping back, "and with a new wardrobe."

"Khalid," she said. "He chose the wardrobe."

"Khalid?" Jake frowned, and then his brow cleared. "You mean, Sheikh Fehr."

She nodded.

"He has good taste," he said.

She nodded again and Jake studied her for an uncomfortable moment. "Were you two really engaged?" he asked.

Liv opened her mouth to say yes, to tell him they'd actually married, but then something in his expression held her back. Jake was afraid for her, afraid of what had happened when she was halfway around the world. "Briefly," she answered, thinking her answer was at least true.

"Is that why you're wearing that enormous ring?"

She'd forgotten all about the yellow diamond and she covered it with her hand, the sharp edges and large stone now so familiar.

"I'm assuming it isn't costume jewelry," Jake added.

Her heart ached all over again. "It's real."

"Your sheikh had a lot of money."

"I couldn't have gotten out of Ozr or Jabal if it weren't for him."

"I'm not criticizing him. I'm grateful."

Her eyes burned and she blinked hard. "Me, too."

Her brother studied her for another long, silent moment. "I'm glad you're back, Liv. We've missed you." He wrapped an arm around her, dropped a kiss on her head. "Now let's get you home. Mom's made dinner and baked you her famous banana buttermilk cake."

Reaching Pierceville, Liv was struck by how green everything was, particularly after her weeks in the desert. It was also humid, which was typical of the south. Fortunately her mom's house was cool and dinner was waiting, along with her mother's homemade cake, which had been a family favorite since Liv was born.

Liv slipped her ring off before dinner and put it in her jewelry box in her room before joining everyone at the table. Even though her mom had lost weight and appeared more frail, she was in great spirits and beamed at Liv throughout dinner.

"My Olivia is home again," she repeated for the fifth time as Jake carried in the cake.

"And not going away anytime soon, I hope," Jake said, placing the cake on the dining room table.

Liv thought of Khalid and his dark eyes and hard features and yet that full sensual mouth that kissed her so tenderly. She pressed her hands together beneath the table. "Nope," she answered, hating the lump that filled her throat. It was what it was, she told herself, and it was over.

But in her room that night Liv couldn't sleep. She didn't know if it was the jet lag or all her pent-up emotions, but sleep eluded her. After an hour of tossing and turning, she gave up. There was no way she was going to sleep, not with her mind racing and that huge, empty feeling inside her and, leaving bed, she headed for the kitchen.

Turning on the kitchen light, Liv opened the refrigerator to pour herself a glass of milk and cut another sliver of her mom's cake. But once she'd cut the cake and had the milk she realized the empty feeling inside her wasn't about food. It was about Khalid.

She missed him. She missed talking to him. She missed his voice. She missed seeing him and having meals with him and most of all missed that hot, electric feeling she got when he looked at her.

If she had his number she'd call him right now. But she didn't have his number and she didn't know how to reach him. She didn't even know where he lived.

The palace in Sarq?

The desert?

Some archaeological dig?

Stabbing her fork into the cake, she tried to ignore how hurt she felt.

He was her husband. He wasn't supposed to send her back. He was supposed to want her with him.

The next month passed exquisitely slowly. Liv dragged herself to work at the travel agency every day and yet, with each passing day, she liked the work less. Most of her customers didn't want to go anywhere. Most of her customers wanted her to book them a room on the Gulf Coast, or a package for four to Disney World. Her customers wanted round-trip air tickets to Chicago for a trade show or, the highlight of her month, an eco-tourism honeymoon to Costa Rica.

But other than that honeymoon trip to Costa Rica, there were no requests for exotic vacations, no interest in ancient ruins, scorching deserts or immense sand dunes shaped by the wind.

As the days passed, she found herself missing the deserts and sand dunes more and more.

She missed Khalid more and more.

When they were in Egypt, she'd been desperate to return to the States, but now that she was back, she didn't know why she'd been so anxious to return. Pierceville was boring. Her job as a travel agent was uninspiring. Her personal life was as empty as could be.

She wanted the colors of Egypt again, the golds and creams and khaki and sand.

She wanted the heat of the desert.

But most of all, she wanted her prince of the desert.

That brief wedding ceremony and the night in his bed had changed something in her heart, had changed the way she thought, felt, breathed. That ceremony had tied them together, united them together, an even though they were now thousands of miles apart she still felt like his, just as he felt like hers.

Her husband. Her hope. Her heart.

Without him, nothing was the same.

The weeks passed and summer was swiftly approaching. Liv's routine was to wake up, go to work, come home and make dinner, do laundry, do errands, go to bed and then wake up the next morning and start over again.

She didn't even mind the work. At least busy—hands typing, cooking, washing, folding—she found she didn't think as much, didn't feel as much. As long as she stayed busy.

Nights…they were another story and Liv had come to dread the night. They were endless. They were dark. They were quiet. And they reminded her of Khalid.

She needed him. She needed to see him. She needed to hear his voice.

She needed him back.

The next morning was Saturday. She had too much time on her hands, and after cleaning the house Liv decided to strip the beds and tackle more laundry. Hauling the sheets downstairs, she turned on the washing machine and started the first load.

"You're getting too thin." It was Jake. He stood in the laundry room doorway watching her.

"I'm fine," she answered briskly, adding the detergent to the wash.

"You're a stick and you don't sleep and you don't eat and you don't smile," he said flatly. "You've been like this ever since you returned from the Middle East."

Looking at her brother, she wondered what he'd say if she told him she'd hoped she'd be pregnant. She wondered how he'd react if she told him she was devastated she wasn't. She wanted Khalid's baby. She wanted him still in her life. She wanted…

"What's going on, Liv?"

"Nothing." She wiped her hands on the back of her shorts and tried to smile.

It was so ridiculous that she wanted to be pregnant. It was so impractical. But she needed Khalid. Not for a baby. But for her. She loved him. Crazy loved him. Couldn't live, think, breathe without him and yet, oh God, how was she to find him, and just go to him, and confess she loved him, and needed him, when he'd been the one to put her in a taxi and send her away?

"You've chewed all your fingernails off and you're wearing a hole in your bedroom carpet with all the pacing you do." Jake's deep voice was quiet, his tone patient. "This isn't the Liv I know."

It wasn't. She wasn't the Liv she knew, either.

Turning to face him, she had tears in her eyes. "Oh, Jake, what am I going to do?"

He leaned against the old door frame. "Do about what?"

"I thought I was pregnant—"

"Hell."

"No. I'm not."

"Praise God."

"No, it's not a miracle, either." She shoved her hands in the pockets of her shorts. "I wanted to be pregnant. I wanted to have his baby."

Understanding dawned in Jake's hazel eyes. "You love your sheikh."

She nodded slowly, tears filling her eyes. "A lot."

"You wanted to be his wife."

"I was." She swallowed hard. "Am. At least I haven't gotten the annulment papers yet."

"Olivia Morse."

She swallowed a second time. "It's actually Princess Olivia Fehr."

"Does Mom know?"

"No!"

"Good. Don't tell her. If she thought you got married without her being there…she'd have a stroke."

Liv sat at her desk, staring at the computer screen. She was supposed to be booking an airline ticket for one of her mother's friends to go see her daughter's new baby. Her mother's friend had just become a grandmother and was excited. Even Liv's mother was excited.

Liv just wanted to go away, far away, but had used all her vacation time for the year. And the following year.

That's when she looked up. And he was there.

In her travel agency. In a gorgeous suit with a white shirt and silk tie looking like a million bucks.

"What…" she said, before breaking off, aware that the agency had gone strangely quiet as all the other travel agents were staring. But of course they'd stare. Khalid Fehr was about the most exotic thing Pierceville had ever seen.

She rolled her chair closer to her desk, leaning forward to demand, "What are you doing here?"

"I need some help planning a trip."

Her lips parted and then she pressed them closed again. Glancing around at the other agents, she forced a small tight smile before gesturing to the chair in front of her desk. "Would you like to sit down?"

"Thank you. That's very kind of you."

She watched him sit down but it wasn't until he was seated across from her that she looked at him properly, really looked at him, and realized his gaze rested on her and only her.

"You've come a long way to get travel advice," she said, nervously straightening the travel brochures and folders littering her desk.

"But you told me you were good."

She stared in fascination at his mouth, and the way the one side curved up in that mocking, rueful way he had and she felt a shiver race through her. God, he was gorgeous, so gorgeous and he'd once been hers, for two days—

Or had he ever been hers?

She frowned, hopelessly confused.

"Where did you want to go?" she asked, striving to be as businesslike as possible.

"I'd like to see the world," he answered.

She tried to hide her bewilderment. "But you've seen a great deal of it already, haven't you?"

"Yes, but this time I'd like to see it all. I was thinking of devoting the next year to traveling around the world."

"That's a lot of traveling," she said, trying to hide her shock.

"There's a lot of world."

She picked up her pen to take notes. "When would you want to leave?"

"Soon."

His matter-of-fact answer made her stomach hurt. "And where would you like to end up?"

"Sarq."

A place she'd never seen, she thought, writing *soon* and *Sarq* on her pad of paper. "And how would you like to travel?"

"By my private jet."

"Right. A nice way to fly. Although I will say flying first class was quite comfortable...." She paused, looked at him. "Thank you for that ticket home."

"My pleasure."

She stared at him for a moment, her temper beginning to rise. "Were you glad to send me home?"

"It's what you wanted."

She opened her mouth to protest but realized he was right. It was what she'd thought she'd wanted. In the beginning. Before she fell in love with him. "What if I hadn't wanted to go home?"

He leaned across the desk. "Then you would have told me."

She couldn't look away from his beautiful face with his dark eyes, eyes that had caught her, captivated her from the first day she met him. "Why are you here?"

"I told you if you ever needed me I'd find you."

Her heart beat a little faster. "Yes."

"And apparently you do need me."

Her heart beat faster still. "Says who?"

"Your brother." The edge of Khalid's mouth lifted ever so slightly. "He wrote me and begged me to get you out of Pierceville. He said it was life and death."

A wash of emotion swept through her. She had to try very hard not to laugh. "Life and death?"

"Apparently so," he answered gravely. "Jake said you're in a terrible place. He said if I don't intervene immediately something bad will happen." Khalid's dark gaze searched hers. "Is that true?"

It was so good, so amazing to see his gorgeous face, to look into those dark soulful eyes, to watch that sexy mouth curve into a smile. "Yes," she whispered, her heart drumming a mile a minute. "It's all true."

"So I have to take action?"

"Yes."

His lashes dropped and his gaze rested on her mouth. "And just what am I saving you from, Princess Fehr?"

Her chest squeezed tight and her throat threatened to close. "A broken heart."

His face was utterly expressionless for a moment and then he smiled, that rare great smile of his, the one that transformed him from rugged into heart-stoppingly beautiful. "You love me."

Tears filled her eyes. "I do, I do, I do."

Suddenly he was around her desk and lifting her to her feet. He clasped her to him, his lips covering hers in a fierce, demanding kiss.

He kissed her until her head spun and her legs buckled and that horrible yawning emptiness inside her started to fill with warmth.

"I love you, my Liv," he said against her mouth. "I love you with all my heart."

"Are you sure?"

"Yes."

"Will you please marry me then?"

He lifted his head, pushed silver-gold strands of hair from her face. "But we are married."

"I know, but my mom doesn't know and she's desperate to have a wedding in the family and then a baby. Her friend Joanne's daughter just had a baby, making her a grandmother—"

Khalid cut her babbling off with another kiss, this one even hotter than the last.

"I think a wedding is a wonderful idea," he said having kissed her senseless. "It's time you met my family."

Aware that every single person in the travel agency was watching them, Liv turned around and, blushing, stammered out an introduction. "Everyone, this is my fiancé, Sheikh Khalid Fehr, and we're getting married."

The travel agents and customers cheered and, cheeks flaming, Liv turned back to Khalid. "So you don't really need travel advice."

He dipped his head, kissed her cheek and then the hollow below her ear. "But I do," he murmured. "I need to know where you want to go for our honeymoon."

"I don't care where we go," she answered, standing on tiptoe to give him another kiss, "as long as we're together."

"Jabal?"

She frowned. "Um, we might be safer in Sarq."

"I think so, too." And, scooping her into his arms, he carried her out of the travel agency. "Tell me you've got a decent hotel in this town," he said as he carried her into the summer sunshine.

She wrapped her arms around his neck. "Nothing special. Sorry."

"Do they have beds?"

Laughing, Liv kissed him. "Yes. But don't you think we should wait for our wedding?" she asked archly.

He growled in her ear, his arms tightening around her. "*No.* Sorry, little one, I've missed you too much. I'm desperate to make you mine again."

EPILOGUE

Later that night...

Liv sat with Khalid and her mom in her mother's living room. "It's going to be a big wedding, Mom," Liv said carefully, not wanting to frighten her mom. "I hope that's okay."

"How big?" her mother asked, still recovering from the shock of learning that Olivia was engaged and getting married to a sheikh quite soon.

"Um, a couple hundred people. Maybe." Liv cringed. "Maybe a few more."

Her mother reached for her glasses and put them on. "And who are all these people we're inviting?"

Liv shot Khalid a please-help-me-now look but he sat back, content to let her battle her way through this one. "Royalty," she said timidly.

Mrs. Morse turned toward her future son-in-law. "Your family."

"Yes," he answered gravely. "My family, along with our friends. Many of whom are royal in their own countries, too."

"I see." Mrs. Morse slid her glasses off and reached for her notebook. "I think we're going to need to increase our budget then."

Liv shot Khalid another desperate glance. "Mom, the Fehr

family would like to help with the wedding. They don't have any daughters and they hoped to put on the wedding…there."

Her mother's eyebrows rose. "*There?* In the desert?"

"Not all of Sarq is desert, Mom. There are cities, beautiful cities—"

"Have you been *there*?" she interrupted.

Liv flushed. Why was her mother doing this now? "No, not to Sarq, not yet, but I've seen pictures, and Khalid's told me."

"Well, that's very nice," Mrs. Morse answered in her best mother voice. "But you are my daughter and we'll do the wedding here."

"Here?"

"In Pierceville."

"Mom, there's no venue big enough!" *Or nice enough*, Liv mentally added.

"But of course there is if we plan an outdoor wedding. We can do something festive. Put up a tent and tables and that sort of thing." Her mother sat tall. "I've seen it done in magazines. There's no reason we can't have a tent and tables and chairs here."

Khalid reached for Liv's hand and kissed it. "I think that's a wonderful idea, Mrs. Morse. We'd love to be married here. And my family, and our friends, will be delighted to come."

"Excellent!" Mrs. Morse rose, beaming. "I'm going to call Joanne. Let her know the good news."

Liv turned on Khalid the moment her mother left the room. "Your family is coming to Pierceville?"

"Why not?"

"Khalid, your brother is a king. Your other brother is a billionaire and international playboy. They'll hate Pierceville."

"They'll love it," he answered, trying hard to check his smile and failing miserably. "Besides, if you get married here, you'll be Pierceville's biggest celebrity for life."

"That's not funny, Khalid!"

He pulled her into his arms, onto his lap and kissed her. "I think it is." He kissed her again, before his expression grew sober. "If it makes your mother happy to have you married here, why not? Where we marry, or where we live, doesn't matter. The only thing I care about is being together."

"That's a great answer."

"It's true."

She clasped his face in her hands, incredibly, hopelessly mad about this man. "I love you, Khalid Fehr, sheikh of the Great Sarq Desert and prince of my heart."

His dark eyes glinted. "Say it again."

"Sheikh of the desert?"

"No, that's a given. The other one."

She touched her lips to his. "You mean, prince of my heart?"

"That's it."

"You are."

"I know." He flashed, grinning wickedly. "I just like hearing it."

* * * * *

THOROUGHBRED LEGACY
*The stakes are high when it comes to love,
horse racing, family secrets
and broken promises.*

*A new exciting Harlequin continuity series coming soon!
Led by* New York Times *bestselling author Elizabeth Bevarly*
FLIRTING WITH TROUBLE

Here's a preview

THE DOOR CLOSED behind them, throwing them into darkness and leaving them utterly alone. And the next thing Daniel knew, he heard himself saying, "Marnie, I'm sorry about the way things turned out in Del Mar."

She said nothing at first, only strode across the room and stared out the window beside him. Although he couldn't see her well in the darkness—he still hadn't switched on a light…but then, neither had she—he imagined her expression was a little preoccupied, a little anxious, a little confused.

Finally, very softly, she said, "Are you?"

He nodded, then, worried she wouldn't be able to see the gesture, added, "Yeah. I am. I should have said goodbye to you."

"Yes, you should have."

Actually, he thought, there were a lot of things he should have done in Del Mar. He'd had *a lot* riding on the Pacific Classic, and even more on his entry, Little Joe, but after meeting Marnie, the Pacific Classic had been the last thing on Daniel's mind. His loss at Del Mar had pretty much ended his career before it had even begun, and he'd had to start all over again, rebuilding from nothing.

He simply had not then and did not now have room in his life for a woman as potent as Marnie Roberts. He was a horseman first and foremost. From the time he was a schoolboy, he'd known what he wanted to do with his life—be the best possible trainer he could be.

He had to make sure Marnie understood—and he understood, too—why things had ended the way they had eight years ago. He just wished he could find the words to do that. Hell, he wished he could find the *thoughts* to do that.

"You made me forget things, Marnie, things that I really needed to remember. And that scared the hell out of me. Little Joe should have won the Classic. He was by far the best horse entered in that race. But I didn't give him the attention he needed and deserved that week, because all I could think about was you. Hell, when I woke up that morning all I wanted to do was lie there and look at you, and then wake you up and make love to you again. If I hadn't left when I did—the way I did— I might still be lying there in that bed with you, thinking about nothing else."

"And would that be so terrible?" she asked.

"Of course not," he told her. "But that wasn't why I was in Del Mar," he repeated. "I was in Del Mar to win a race. That was my job. And my work was the most important thing to me."

She said nothing for a moment, only studied his face in the darkness as if looking for the answer to a very important question. Finally she asked, "And what's the most important thing to you now, Daniel?"

Wasn't the answer to that obvious? "My work," he answered automatically.

She nodded slowly. "Of course," she said softly. "That is, after all, what you do best."

Her comment, too, puzzled him. She made it sound as if being good at what he did was a bad thing.

She bit her lip thoughtfully, her eyes fixed on his, glimmering in the scant moonlight that was filtering through the window. And damned if Daniel didn't find himself wanting to pull her into his arms and kiss her. But as much as it might have felt as if no time had passed since Del Mar, there were eight years between now and then. And eight years was a long time in the best of circumstances. For Daniel and Marnie, it was virtually a lifetime.

So Daniel turned and started for the door, then halted. He couldn't just walk away and leave things as they were, unsettled. He'd done that eight years ago and regretted it.

"It *was* good to see you again, Marnie," he said softly. And since he was being honest, he added, "I hope we see each other again."

She didn't say anything in response, only stood silhouetted against the window with her arms wrapped around her in a way that made him wonder whether she was doing it because she was cold, or if she just needed something—someone—to hold on to. In either case, Daniel understood. There was an emptiness clinging to him that he suspected would be there for a long time.

* * * * *

THOROUGHBRED LEGACY
coming soon wherever books are sold!

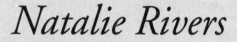

I ♥

HARLEQUIN® *Presents*

BROUGHT TO YOU BY FANS OF
HARLEQUIN PRESENTS.

We are its editors and authors
and biggest fans––and we'd
love to hear from YOU!

Subscribe today to our online blog at
www.iheartpresents.com

REQUEST YOUR FREE BOOKS!

2 FREE NOVELS PLUS 2 FREE GIFTS!

PASSION GUARANTEED SEDUCTION

YES! Please send me 2 FREE Harlequin Presents® novels and my 2 FREE gifts (gifts are worth about $10). After receiving them, if I don't wish to receive any more books, I can return the shipping statement marked "cancel". If I don't cancel, I will receive 6 brand-new novels every month and be billed just $4.05 per book in the U.S. or $4.74 per book in Canada, plus 25¢ shipping and handling per book and applicable taxes, if any*. That's a savings of close to 15% off the cover price! I understand that accepting the 2 free books and gifts places me under no obligation to buy anything. I can always return a shipment and cancel at any time. Even if I never buy another book, the two free books and gifts are mine to keep forever.

106 HDN ERRW   306 HDN ERRL

Name	(PLEASE PRINT)	
Address		Apt. #
City	State/Prov.	Zip/Postal Code

Signature (if under 18, a parent or guardian must sign)

Mail to the **Harlequin Reader Service**:
IN U.S.A.: P.O. Box 1867, Buffalo, NY 14240-1867
IN CANADA: P.O. Box 609, Fort Erie, Ontario L2A 5X3

Not valid to current subscribers of Harlequin Presents books.

Want to try two free books from another line?
Call 1-800-873-8635 or visit www.morefreebooks.com.

HARLEQUIN *Presents*

Don't forget Harlequin Presents EXTRA
now brings you a powerful new collection
every month featuring four books!

Be sure not to miss any of the titles in

In the Greek Tycoon's Bed,

available May 13:

THE GREEK'S FORBIDDEN BRIDE
by Cathy Williams

THE GREEK TYCOON'S UNEXPECTED WIFE
by Annie West

THE GREEK TYCOON'S VIRGIN MISTRESS
by Chantelle Shaw

THE GIANNAKIS BRIDE
by Catherine Spencer

EXTRA

TALL, DARK AND SEXY

The men who never fail—seduction included!

Brooding, successful and arrogant, these men
can sweep any female they desire off her feet.
But now there's only one woman they want—
and they'll use their wealth, power, charm and
irresistibly seductive ways to claim her!

**Don't miss any of the titles in this exciting
collection available June 10, 2008:**

#9 THE BILLIONAIRE'S VIRGIN BRIDE
by HELEN BROOKS

#10 HIS MISTRESS BY MARRIAGE
by LEE WILKINSON

#11 THE BRITISH BILLIONAIRE AFFAIR
by SUSANNE JAMES

#12 THE MILLIONAIRE'S
MARRIAGE REVENGE
by AMANDA BROWNING

*Harlequin Presents EXTRA delivers a themed
collection every month featuring 4 new titles.*

www.eHarlequin.com   HPE0608